148
Charles
Street

A Novel

TRACY DAUGHERTY

University of Nebraska Press   Lincoln

The University of Nebraska Press is part of a land-
grant institution with campuses and programs on the
past, present, and future homelands of the Pawnee,
Ponca, Otoe-Missouria, Omaha, Dakota, Lakota, Kaw,
Cheyenne, and Arapaho Peoples, as well as those of the
relocated Ho-Chunk, Sac and Fox, and Iowa Peoples.

Library of Congress Cataloging-in-Publication Data
Names: Daugherty, Tracy, author.
Title: 148 Charles Street: a novel / Tracy Daugherty.
Description: Lincoln: University of Nebraska Press, [2022]
Identifiers: LCCN 2021040772
ISBN 9781496229748 (paperback)
ISBN 9781496231703 (epub)
ISBN 9781496231710 (pdf)
Subjects: LCSH: Cather, Willa, 1873–1947—Fiction. |
Sergeant, Elizabeth Shepley, 1881–1965—Fiction. | BISAC:
FICTION / Literary | FICTION / Historical /
General | LCGFT: Biographical fiction.
Classification: LCC PS3554.A85 A614
2022 | DDC 813/.54—dc23
LC record available at https://lccn.loc.gov/2021040772

Set in Garamond Premier Pro by Mikala R. Kolander
Designed by L. Auten.

For Margie, for Jon and Maryann

Virtue is concerned with action; art with production.

—ARISTOTLE

The problem in life is to harmonize these two.

—ANNIE FIELDS

ACKNOWLEDGMENTS

My thanks to Roger Angell, who was always very kind to me, if (I think) a little irritated at my callowness. In our many exchanges and conversations, we never spoke of his aunt, Elsie Sergeant, though when I later discovered he was her nephew, it made perfect sense to me. I felt I got to know a bit of her through him.

Sidney Wade was splendid company in Red Cloud. George Manner's ghost will forever be my guide to Santa Fe. Suzanne Berne has always been the consummate Boston hostess. God bless New York for being New York.

Patricia Lee Yongue introduced me to the work of Willa Cather at the University of Houston. The seeds of this novel were planted in her classroom nearly forty years ago.

I am grateful to Abigail Goodwin, Rosemary Sekora, and Stephanie Ward for their efforts on my behalf.

This book would never have seen the light of day without the enthusiasm and help of Clark Whitehorn at the University of Nebraska Press. I am deeply grateful to him—and to the press—for being such an attentive caretaker of Cather's legacy.

148
Charles
Street

Prologue

On Charles Street, in the Beacon Hill area of Boston, in 1908, the Massachusetts Eye and Ear Infirmary broke ground on the construction of a dormitory for its nurses. It would be erected near the old tidal flats in the Back Bay and a bend in the Charles River where swan boats creased the currents. The venerable architectural firm Page and Frothingham envisioned a multistory Georgian Revival building whose imposing presence would require the demolition of several family dwellings, many fashioned in the Federal and Victorian styles of the previous two centuries with mansard roofs and gabled eaves. It would be necessary, as well, to destroy the homes' modest carriage houses and small vegetable gardens.

Most of the neighborhood's residents considered the appearance of the dormitory an ill omen for Charles Street, a threat to the health of remaining older structures: they feared that real estate prices would rise and erode ancient establishments. The medical facility had loosed a landslide toward the commercialization of the avenue, people said, bringing with it an inevitable falling-off from the past—a loss of civility apparent in folks' faster rhythms, fewer lingering conversations in open-air markets.

In point of fact, Charles Street had always served as a commercial hub for the region. The scattered family lots along the road were much rarer than newly erected rows of shops, whose owners insisted that the community flourished more readily as a result of their financial negotiations. That the past had been continuously in the process of vanishing, locally, was evident in the absence of the three peaks that had once given the place its name—Trimountain, a marker later changed to Beacon Hill, after Mount Vernon had been leveled by fifty to sixty feet for development purposes, followed by the pick-axing of Pemberton Hill and the humbling of Beacon in order to thicken the mud flats beside the river. The flats formed a smooth ravine for Charles Street at the western foot of the hill. Economic growth had long replaced natural forces—the appearance of accident—as the immediate driver of local evolution. If, in 1908, certain families believed the nurses' domicile signaled a radical shift in the area's building practices (a charge the Beacon Hill Civic Association's Zoning and Licensing Committee firmly denied), it was because these families had become inured, after two or three generations, to the high leaded windows of luxury antique stores, the sooty brick fronts of private meeting halls, the stained purple glass of well-adorned Christian churches. Massachusetts Eye and Ear had existed as a neighborhood mainstay since its founding as a free clinic in 1824.

One sleety, cold March day, during the early phase of the dormitory's progress, one of the Charles Street strollers noted the wooden spires—visible one moment, immaterial the next depending on one's position with respect to the sun, the changing slant of light. She was petite, dressed in a long wool coat, plum-colored with a thick beige ostrich collar. She wore a pointed gray hat topped with a modest turquoise peacock feather. The smile rounding her cheeks revealed the pleasure she took in her outrageous costuming—outrageous because she had been prairie-raised, most comfortable as a girl clothed in mud, dirt, and faint grass stains, resembling fine fabric prints, on her skin. She dressed up to cheer herself on this day of winter dregs, in this strange and teeming city that never seemed to find its natural pace, block to block, under constant hammering and digging. The air smelled of oiled machine smoke and the coffee grounds in back of the many breakfast cafés. In the distance, bright white elms hovered over the river like slender lighthouse towers made of twigs and leaves.

To Willa Cather, tugging her plum coat tighter at her waist, the greatness of Charles Street did not depend on the numbers

of apothecaries, of knitting or tobacco shops, versus the further-
ance of quaint family homes here; the lane's value rested solely
on a single narrow three-story house set on a tidy lawn stretching
to the banked black lip of the river's shore. Sometimes from the
street—depending on the red velvet curtains, drawn or not drawn
in the tiered windows—one could glimpse the rare books in the
second-floor library, their rough leather spines, and, filling the
front parlor, the polished black top of the grand piano, propped
high, reflecting sunlight back into the sky. Always, approaching
the house, Willa squinted to see at what distance she could first
ascertain interior details, within how many steps of the Park Street
Church (a "felicitous refuge" in the words of Henry James—James
had once been a regular guest in the house she was hurrying to visit);
she wondered if her gaze could penetrate the windows from the
burial ground adjacent to King's Chapel, where the name Elizabeth
Pain chiseled in a chipped granite stone inspired Hawthorne to
imagine the life of Hester Prynne, whom he discussed, perhaps,
in quietly tragic tones, in the parlor of the cherished house now
coming into Willa's view.

The vanished past did not trouble her overmuch, not on this
day at least, not while she remained cloaked in her costume and
her vigorous youth—though recently one of the house's gracious
inhabitants had complained that, since the advent of the motor-
car, Charles Street belonged only to the quick and the dead. That
the time of Hawthorne and James, of so many others—Whitman,
Emerson, Longfellow—was finished paled beside the fact that such
men had once supped within these walls. (Dickens was said to have
served strong, sweet punch one night at a party and to have led
the dancing—"Reels! Set!" he called to men and women prancing
across the parquet floors.) Willa's presence here now meant that she
had been welcomed into their company. The writers' voices had not
ceased: they were sealed inside the books in the second-floor library.
One day, soon, she would add a book to their glorious volumes and
join the house's continuing conversation.

The only disturbances hindering her happiness on this windy March morning were visions of white-clad nurses bustling up the street, jostling other passersby in their haste to reach Eye and Ear, and the sour recollection of her last house visit, when she had introduced her clumsy New York friend to the estate's grand dames. In truth, it was not the imagined glut of medical assistants hoarding sidewalk space that pained her—a mild ache in her temples—it was what they represented. Illness. Infirmity. She could not bear the possibility that some disabling calamity might strike her out of the blue (it could happen!) before she finished her book and took her rightful place within the sedate, fire-lit rooms of 148 Charles Street.

As for her young friend Elsie, Willa could barely forgive her— snickering behind her hand, that afternoon, at the curl of Keats's hair preserved under glass on a mantel in the library, smiling as the old ladies recalled Dickens's eloquence, his personal charm. Later, she had whispered to Willa in the parlor, "I think our dears fell head over heels for the father of Little Nell." Perhaps Willa should have known better than to bring Elsie here; the girl had a reckless weakness for social reform—just like the rest of her silly Bryn Mawr classmates—an impulse impairing her writing, Willa thought: her sentences were hard, polemical bleats. Naturally, Elsie would find the real story of Charles Street in its economic transformation rather than in what she called the "dowagers' literary mausoleum." When Willa expressed her abhorrence at this cruel characterization, Elsie cried, "Really, I'm astonished at you! How can you feel at home in such a dark and stultified atmosphere? I have to tell you, all day today I felt our hostesses were trying to tone you down, to freeze you into their stiff manners, and you—whether you were aware of it or not—rightly resisted, a wild, spirited colt." She laughed. "Honestly, you blew into the place like a fresh wind from your prairie, and none of their dusty old trinkets could withstand the force of your gale!"

What Elsie failed to appreciate, in her zeal for The New, was the steady breeze of Tradition, Willa thought now, the artist's need to release her voice into that generating current, to link with it, discover direction from it, strengthening her natural powers. Reform, reform: Elsie's tiresome battle cry. Her prayer. But some things—objects, ideas, frail human appurtenances—required protection from time's depredations: the poet's lock of hair.

And yes, oh yes—the past would vanish. Oh my dear, of course it would. Years ago, when Willa first saw Wagner's *Ring*, overwhelmed by the operatic cycle—exactly as the composer intended—she believed, from now on, singers would perform Brünnhilde's triumphs and tragedies on the world's great stages. "Gesamtkunstwerk," Wagner had proclaimed—"a total work of art." But now his innovations had been dismissed as dated by theatrical reformers, insisting on "aesthetic distance" and "social relevance" as art's latest currency. The New quickly became The Old, stranding artists committed to a worn-out style as hopelessly as Brünnhilde on a windswept crag, surrounded by rings of fire. Elsie did not understand this. Willa's stiffened peacock feather was no guard from the gloom she kept just barely at bay most days. Hawthorne knew. So did James. 148 Charles Street was the "ark of the modern deluge," James had observed on one of his last lingering calls here. And Hawthorne—splendid, melancholy soul!—grieving all his losses in advance, once lamented, "One of my choicest ideal places in the world is this warm little drawing room on Charles Street, and therefore I seldom visit it."

Book One

Tesuque, 1922

I

On the third day of work on the mud hut, Elsie's wounded leg gave
way and she went spiraling down the eastern slope of a reddish
sandstone arroyo, past black slashes of pine limbs, cactus, and spiky
sage growths. The breath fled her chest as she barreled over pebbles
and twigs. *Elasticity is a property of time*: a Pueblo man had offered
this observation at her dinner table in a Santa Fe hotel just last
night. As a fleeting impression, she felt the truth of his assertion
now, rolling through a cloud of fine white powder rising from the
dirt, plugging her nostrils, smearing grit across her thin, chapped
lips. *Too alkaline*, she thought, tasting the soil. Then she registered
the fact that, in the midst of her distress, a quiet corner of her mind
was busy contemplating—as if it could stretch time at its will—the
hill's steepness.

An irony: she might not be in such danger now if, months
ago, she had not chosen this spot for its slope. She had believed
its gentle terraces made it more fertile than the other lots she'd
considered buying. Elsewhere, where more ruined adobes awaited
salvation, juniper, greasewood, and Spanish bayonets clotted the
rocky ground, but here, in the blue shadows of the Sangre de Cris-
tos, stunted acacias and apple tree roots signaled lush possibilities
in spite of the alkali. All it would take was a little work, enriching
the deep, carnelian soil.

Now—rolling, rolling—time, or her perception of time, wobbled
further. In mental flashes, she heard a man's faint, croaking voice,
a flat Oklahoma accent, begging, "Water, water!" She understood
that her mind had returned to the American Hospital in Paris.
There, four years ago, wondering if her leg would ever heal—cries

of "water, water" from the dying soldier in the next bed—she had first longed for the circumstances that sent her flying down this hill today: an incalculably large blue sky and a desert big enough to tuck all of Europe into its pocket.

Elsie thumped to a halt in a narrow shale cleft at the bottom of the arroyo, pelted by clods and thorns. Her left ankle became the center of all life. It throbbed into orbit somewhere just above the rest of her body, a pure streak of pain dislodged from her physical being. It swelled to fill the world. She may have lost consciousness for a moment or just the opposite: *become* the rocks and trees. A hissing trickle . . . the blood in her ears? Then she feared she was hearing the approach of small fanged animals preparing to tear the organs from her carcass. A low, gravelly voice—a man's—reached her as if through a hole in the earth: "Here, now. Lie still. I've got you."

Got her he had: groping hands at the base of her buttocks, beneath her right armpit, where the swell of her breast seemed to center another source of pain, the near-impossibility of breath, and then the raw pressure, welcome though it was, of air returning to her lungs. Just before she passed out, sunlight burned her eyes, silhouetting what appeared to be a massive bald head hovering above her, a slate-colored face expressing only shadows.

She woke in a cool adobe room, amber walls close around her, cozy not stifling, a single wedge of light shimmering somewhere to her left, nearly at eye level, yellow then white then yellow once more: the fluttering of a sheer lace curtain. A vinegar smell, alcohol—pungent. The gravelly voice: "It's okay. Relax. I've brought you to the doctor."

Water, water. Where was she? Maybe it *was* the American Hospital. Her consciousness came and went. Men's voices. (Were they real?) Was she the only woman in the world? "We must cut off your clothes, Madame. Forgive me." "Is it serious?" "The left foot? Yes. Very." Hands tied to a table. Green plaster ceiling. "For now, I will leave the small wounds on your face, yes? How do you suppose I could touch up anything so delicate as the face of a woman? That is not what we do here." All she could think was, *So this is how you die.* White curtains, white cushions, white chairs. Blue figures—scowling male nurses smelling of blood and iodine—moving among rolling silver tables topped with gleaming instruments. The boy dying next to her, whispering *water, water* . . . no, no, this was *her* voice now, begging for drink; *she* was the one who was parched, *she* was struggling for life . . . she'd traveled years beyond the sick room in Paris. Years.

She'd come to Tesuque. How long ago? She was in Tesuque *now.* She lay in a cool adobe room: there *was* no plaster ceiling, no soldier dying next to her. She'd been working on her hut—yes, just this afternoon—when something happened. Her ankle! That *ripped* feeling, a liquid burst of engorgement. It was exactly the same in the Marne, on the battlefield—when was it? Four years ago? She didn't know, but she could still recall the moment her silly companion said, "What is this? A German prayer book?" And then the scorching orange bloom, the lieutenant's stringy voice: "My arm, my arm . . . it's been carried away!"

Distant now. Nothing to do with today. Her ankle may have shattered again, but this was an entirely different situation. Yes. She must focus. Clear her head. Anchor herself. The adobe room. The hut. What just happened at the hut?

"My dear, what a spill you took! Do you remember rolling down the hill? I got to you as quickly as I could." She blinked twice, hard. A round head, hairless, a couple of shiny divots right above the ears, the whole comical arrangement popping out of a clerical collar. A trace of whiskey on the man's heavy breath.

"Who are you?" Elsie managed to ask. "Can I have some water?"

"Frederick. Frederick Courvaille."

"A priest?"

He nodded. Was his presence here cause for alarm?

Another man, a smaller fellow dressed in smudged khaki pants and a white chemise, edged into her line of sight between the wedge of light and faint shadows cast by piñon beams above her. He gripped a glass and a clear pitcher of water. She drank.

"This is Dr. Gonzalez," said Father Courvaille. "He'll take good care of you."

Behind the doctor, a swarthy woman wearing a brown cotton dress and a floured apron dithered near the light—a small window, Elsie saw now. The woman, doll-like in her tiny proportions, frowned at her.

The doctor set the pitcher on the floor. Elsie realized she was lying on a low wooden table in the middle of an otherwise bare room. Her blouse had been partially unbuttoned. Sweat pooled like syrup in the hollow of her neck. Cold. She felt a draft below her waist. Tenderly, the man lifted her exposed left leg. The ankle screamed its silent scream. With blunt fingertips the doctor traced the white scars raised across the unshaved surface of her calf, just below her knee. He lifted his brows—bushy caterpillars. He wanted to know about the scars.

"The war," Elsie explained, her head slowly clearing. "In France. Four years ago." She noticed her pants tossed unceremoniously into a cobwebbed corner of the room. *We must cut off your clothes, Madame.* "I was a reporter. Covering the fighting for a magazine. One day . . . an accident . . . a fellow reporter, another woman . . . stupidly, she picked up . . ." She shut her eyes.

The doctor settled her leg on the table. "And the ankle?" he said. "It was badly damaged at that time?"

"Both ankles, but especially the left. Shrapnel. It's still very weak. I guess that's why I slipped today while working on the hill."

The doctor nodded. "You have broken a small bone in the inner foot, here." He pressed a spot just above her instep. A sting: like wasps—forty, fifty of them, tucked inside her muscles. "I will wrap it and you must keep weight off this foot for at least three weeks."

The meaty priest loitered above her head, the flesh of his chin bristling with whiskers. "I have a cane I can lend you," he said. "Several, in fact. You'll have your choice of many fine artifacts!"

Elsie noticed he limped as he circled the table. It couldn't have been easy for him to carry her here. "You see, I am a connoisseur of lameness."

The doctor bandaged her foot, offered her more water, and then, blushing, handed over her clothes. Father Courvaille steadied her against his shoulder while she pulled the pants past her ankle.

She tried to take a step toward the doorway. The scowling woman waved her doll-arms at the window. "Miguel! Miguel!" she called to the doctor. Her familiarity, her contempt for the man, suggested he was her husband. He moved to see what she was pointing at. Just then, the prolonged exhale of a shotgun blast, somewhere nearby, shook Elsie's ribs; her injured foot hit the floor. The ankle seemed to crumple, like crêpe paper. An inhuman shriek followed the sound of the shot: dry wood splintering in several directions, chips pelting the house, the window's tea-colored panes.

The doctor unlocked his window. "Bastards!" he shouted. Father Courvaille pulled Elsie across the room, hobbling, nearly falling, away from the open center. Together, they cowered behind the doctor's shoulder, peering out along with his wife. Three Pueblo men, wearing felt hats black as little terriers, lingered by the barbed-wire fence surrounding the adobe's small yard. They aimed rifles at the oak posts. Wire sagged to the dirt. Fence fragments pierced the trunk of a cottonwood bent leafless in the yard.

"Can you hear me in there? This ain't the voice of no friendly burning bush!" yelled the tallest intruder. "This ain't no act of God! We told you last week—told you straight: if you didn't remove this fence, we'd take it down for you!"

"This land is mine," answered the doctor.

"No. Our governor grants you the house for lease, since you do your healing there," the man said. Behind him, his partners spoke softly in Tewa. "But the property around it—paper, voice, and parchment say it's *ours*! Make this fence disappear—erase it from the Earth right now, you hear me?—and we got no trouble."

"I have a patient in here!" the doctor protested.

After a minute, the speaker convinced his men to lower their guns. "All right, Healer. We'll give you one more day. But tomorrow we're back here and we'd better not find this fence!"

The men shouldered their rifles and slipped away through the white elms beyond the drooping wire. The elms' spindly limbs trembled with mistletoe.

Two days later, Father Courvaille sat with Elsie in what would one day be the kitchen of her hut. Now it was merely a rough staked-out rectangle, dirt mixed with a little caliche at the top of the hill, covered with a tarp. Elsie had asked the priest to set up two maple chairs in the shade. Over an open fire she brewed English tea. Horse-flies swirled above the copper kettle until it whistled. Like a rain of pebbles, the vibrating insect swarm scattered down the hillside.

Golden poplars and pale cottonwoods ringed the hut's western perimeter, defining the edge of the gouge among sand hummocks and rocks forming the Acequia Madre. A faint sulfur smell rose from the braiding brown water. Swift-moving mare's-tail clouds brushed the midday sun.

Elsie asked Father Courvaille if he knew what had happened to Dr. Gonzalez's fence. Last night, in the lobby of the Santa Fe hotel where she spent certain evenings—it was thirty miles south of Tesuque—she had read in the *Santa Fe New Mexican* that the "peoples of the Tesuque Pueblo" appeared to be "on the warpath." "I thought it highly unfair, not to mention racially prejudiced, for the editors to characterize the conflict that way," she said.

"Ah yes, but you *would* think it unfair, wouldn't you?" said the priest. He blew on his steaming cup. A pattern of painted pink daisies graced its rim. "You and the other Eastern ladies." He said this lightly, as if making a joke. "You've invaded us here, bearing tart New England wisdom for improving our lives." He laughed.

"Busybodies?" Elsie smiled at him. "Is that how you see us? Forgive me, Father, but that's just as narrow-minded as 'Indians on the warpath.'" His clumsy manner made her nervous. It would be a long afternoon.

"But I *am* curious. How did this . . . exodus? influx? . . . begin?" he asked. "I must tell you, the recent rush of so many strangers has excited the gossips here. Everyone wonders what these women are doing together, huddling all alone in the woods."

Elsie ignored his probing innuendo.

"When I saw you take your tumble the other day, I was on my way here to introduce myself to you, to try to get to know you a little . . . to . . . well . . . to understand . . ."

"I can't speak for the women I assume you're referring to—the ladies who've restored those old huts on the mesas north of us here?"

He nodded. "I confess, whenever I meet them in the plaza in town, they're rather cool to me."

"I don't know them very well, though we were all classmates—at roughly the same time, a few years ago—at Bryn Mawr," Elsie explained. "Our professors there taught us to aspire to 'something splendid' with our lives and to pursue our ambitions—whatever they may be. We were trained not to dismiss our desires as 'inappropriately feminine.'"

"And so," said the priest, "moving out west, purchasing land, redoing primitive dwellings—this is all to prove that your femininity is no impediment to dreaming big?" He pointed at her bandaged foot. "Is that why you went to war?"

"Are you mocking me, Father Courvaille?"

"Not at all. I am, as I say, genuinely curious."

"The others would have their own stories to tell. Their particular reasons. It's true I'm here partly because of their example. I'd heard of their desert adventures through friends of friends back east, and the details . . . well, they excited me. I am, after all, a writer, a reporter, and it pleases me to document new experiences. 'In the West, there is more color in five minutes than in fifty years in the East,' I was told. I was informed the roads here are what the French call *intime*. Friendly. Intimate. But mainly I came because of my friend Willa Cather."

The priest, surprised at the name, spilled a little tea. "The novelist?"

"The same."

"You know her?"

"She's been a mentor to me. It was she who told me this was the most beautiful country she had ever seen, like the stretch between Marseilles and Nice only much more brilliant. Here. Let me show you." She rose with a groan, waving off the man's move to assist her. She snatched up the silver-headed oak cane he had lent her two days ago before driving her, in his parish's flatbed truck, from Dr. Gonzalez's clinic to her Santa Fe hotel. (The priest suffered from gout.) In the truck, he'd told her the cane resembled the power sticks the Pueblo governors raised whenever they directed community meetings—meetings convened to discuss alleged land grabs by Anglos and Mexican farmers.

Elsie bump-bumped into a small dusty room inside the hut, pushing aside scattered lumber that would soon—if her workers returned!—shore up new ceilings. From atop a crude pinewood bookshelf, adorned with beads and polished rocks, she plucked a blue-and-green peacock feather.

Shuffling back outside—invigorated by a woody scent in the air, like incense and acorn; oh, the unexpected gifts of this place!—she said to the priest, "Before I show you . . . Dr. Gonzalez's fence?"

"Oh yes." She had caught him crouching over his chair, tucking a tiny silver flask into a back pocket as big as a mail carrier's pouch. A smell as of turpentine or oil now drifted from his cup. "As far as I know, it remains intact, except for the damage we witnessed the other day. The good doctor has been granted a temporary reprieve by the Pueblo. All sides have agreed to mediation. Our congressman is arranging a session."

"Well." Elsie settled into her chair. The cane dropped to her side. "I was worried about him. And unlike the ladies we were just discussing—who all spring, more or less, from wealth—I'm self-supporting, freelancing for magazines. Perhaps impulsively, I sank most of my savings into this property. Candidly, I don't know how I'll pay the doctor ..."

"I'll ask him to be patient with you."

Elsie smiled at him, more genuinely this time. She held the feather up to the wind. "From one of Willa's hats. She gave it to me on a special occasion, as a kind of good luck charm. She said it would protect me."

The priest took the feather from her hand, riffling the airy edges. His fingers trembled.

"Her hat was made in Paris," Elsie said, "where all the *best* hats are made, according to Willa."

"I appreciated her evocations of our western canyons in her novel about the opera singer," said Father Courvaille.

"*The Song of the Lark.* Yes. In *my* view, Willa first found her voice in that book. She loves the Southwest as much as she loves France—or the idea of France as it used to be. One of the reasons I treasure this feather ... Willa offered it to me as I was about to sail for Europe to cover the war." When war broke out, Willa had reacted very differently than Elsie to news of the battles. Elsie knew she had to go, to see directly what was happening to her beloved Paris. Willa, she remembered, couldn't bear to consider the devastation. She was miserable. "Our present is ruined—but we had such a beautiful past," she wept. The only thing that cheered her that day, the day Elsie came to tell her goodbye before boarding the ship, was the Pueblo and Hopi pottery she'd bought here, years earlier. She'd arranged the pots on a mantel in her Greenwich Village apartment—turned them so they'd catch the afternoon sun. The pots, the memories they contained of her travels in New Mexico, gave her such pleasure.

Elsie squirmed: a twinge in her ankle. "Her reverence for this place stayed with me throughout my ordeals in the Marne," she said to the priest. "As I was recovering from my injuries, in the American

Hospital, I dreamed of retreating here, away from the shouting and machinery. Peaceful isolation. I kept hearing Willa's voice, praising the desert. 'A landscape of *sky*!' she'd say. When I returned to the States, a doctor in New York affirmed that the high, dry atmosphere near Santa Fe would benefit my health. My mind was made up."

"I don't suppose you can expect a visit from your friend?" asked the priest. "I'd dearly love to meet the great lady."

Elsie laughed. "Yes, she *is* a great lady," and she *would* soon appear—not physically, but rather in the shape of her latest novel, a copy of which she was arranging to mail to Elsie, according to a note Elsie had received yesterday at the hotel. Willa was now calling the book *One of Ours*. Her war story. Elsie dreaded reading it.

She didn't tell the priest she was expecting a second arrival in the weeks ahead, the thought of which disturbed her as much as Willa's book, though she didn't quite know why. She loved Dr. Jung, and he was coming all the way from Europe. Her recent letters to him, cataloging myths and visions of the Southwest natives, had apparently fascinated him. Perhaps she feared that the stories, once he heard them face-to-face, wouldn't match her inspiring descriptions of them. Perhaps his presence, gentle though it was, would carry with it whiffs of sadder days. After all, hadn't she moved west in order to escape the wreck of Europe?

The priest sipped his tea. "I admire your ambition," he said, nodding at the hut's sagging north wall. "Though I confess I don't know how you're going to manage the work around here with your affliction."

"You've been very kind these last two days. Attentive," Elsie said. "Or is it simply that you don't think a woman can get along on her own?" She smiled broadly—not without growing ease with the man.

"Oh, please don't mistake my questioning, my quibbling, for criticism. Or skepticism. Or suspicion or anything of the sort."

"But?"

He grinned. "Do you really think this place is *worth* saving?"

"I've discovered in the past few weeks, Father, that vastness, open skies have far more appeal to me than the enclosed mountain valleys of the East." Besides, she said, she was charmed by the history of her little hut—at least what the realtor in Santa Fe had told her about it. He said a young *charro* had built it for his bride, offering her sturdy walls since the power of her kiss had crumbled the walls of his heart.

"I should warn you, my dear, not to view life here through the filter of romance. I saw a Mexican boy in my parish approach a pretty *muchacha* after Mass one day. 'Violeta, will you marry me?' he asked. She answered, 'No.' He pulled out a pistol, shot her in the head, then killed himself right beside her in the road."

Elsie shivered, banging her foot on a chair.

"I'm sorry," said Father Courvaille. "I shouldn't speak so harshly. It's just that . . . lives are hard here. People are poor. And I fear that you and your friends from Boston and New York . . . well, frankly, Miss Sergeant, I worry about your misconceptions. 'Nobility through suffering' and the like. You see, I've read some of your journalism."

"Have you, now?"

"*The Nation* is not unknown to us here. We're not quite as backward as we seem." He smiled. "I've done my homework. You're what we'd call a reformer."

"Father, it was the United States Supreme Court, in one of its rulings not long ago, that called this nation's indigenous population 'essentially a simple, uninformed and inferior people.' I make no apologies for working to change that perception."

"But here's my question, young lady, and please don't take it ill. Why is it incumbent upon you to come to this place—an alien place to you, however much you cherish its colors and textures—to support a foreign culture?"

"Father Courvaille." Elsie spoke quietly. The fire on which she had brewed the tea had fallen into ash. "I've just witnessed the grand old cultures of Europe nearly destroyed. Perhaps they *have* been damaged beyond salvaging. We'll see if those countries will recover. The experience . . . well, it made me rethink *our* country." She paused to find the right words. "It's my belief that, if America is to be great, it must have a culture of its own—not a second-rate, hand-me-down culture inherited from the Old World, a poor relation of England or France. A culture as naturally and firmly rooted as that strong young apple tree over there. And, in fact, we *do* have such a culture." She gestured at the shallow canyon. "It's here. And it *is* worth saving."

"Well, you *are* a wordsmith," said Father Courvaille. "Your mentor, Miss Cather, taught you well."

It troubled Elsie, this casual comparison to Willa. We're not *at all* alike, she wanted to say. "It must give you great solace to attend the needs of your parish," she said instead, evading the subject.

He laughed. "Miss Sergeant, the members of my parish—I know them well; I'm one of them—they need money. They need physical comfort. They need entertainment. What they don't need is a do-gooder's prattling or—forgive me—reform. Or more precisely: reformers with naive intentions. As for me . . ." He glanced at her piercingly. He seemed to have made a bold decision on the spot. He half stood, pulled the silver flask from his back pocket, and made a great show of adding alcohol to the last of his tea. "I find solace in whiskey. I don't mind confessing to you that, in many ways, I am not a very good priest."

As he spoke, she remembered the feel of his groping hands on her body the day he lifted her, broken, from the bottom of the arroyo. She didn't know precisely why—his bumbling, perhaps, his harmless flailing—but she sensed he was not a bad man. Not a predator. No. As his flask flashed whitely in the sun, she thought she saw him for what he was: a sloppy, undisciplined old fellow snatching worldly pleasures wherever he could.

"My value, here, lies in my similarities to those I serve," he said. "The flaws I share with them. Otherwise, I would not be able to truly grasp the concept of forgiveness. I would not be able to pass on to them God's grace." He threw back his head and drained the rest of his tea. "And now I should take my leave. I fear you feel you've sat through a sermon." He laughed. "Actually, I only intended to welcome you today, to make sure you were well."

"Thank you," Elsie said. "I'm glad for your visit."

"I'll leave you with a local blessing: 'May San Antonio protect the night from all insects!' And here, let me help you." He stooped to retrieve her cane. He placed it in her lap. "This is one of my favorites. Do you know . . . Abraham Lincoln once ordered hundreds of canes made, just like this one. He gifted these splendid objects to the peoples of New Mexico."

"Why?" Elsie asked.

"See the Moorish design etched into the head here, the old European styling right below the shape of the eagle? These canes were covenants to the Indians—reminders of the days when the Pueblos were wards of the Spanish crown, retaining full rights to their lands. Complete sovereignty—though of course it hasn't always worked out that way. Lincoln promised to honor that ancient agreement. And he did. These canes were his handshake."

With great effort Elsie stood, leveraging the thick oak stick. "And so, in the matter of Dr. Gonzalez's fence, you come down on the side of the Pueblos?"

A white-throated bird fluttered, at the edge of the tarp, in ruby sunlight.

"I take no sides. I just know that whoever has the most guns will win."

Elsie listened to a distant drone of locusts. "It strikes me, Father, that you've a rather dour view of human behavior—for a priest."

"My dear, who else *but* a priest to look askance at humanity's sins and the sadness they bring to the world?" For an instant, his bitter smile seemed to burden his furrowed being.

2

That evening, after Father Courvaille had left, Elsie spread her pallet on the floor of the hut. She had decided not to return to Santa Fe, to the room held in her name. Her left foot would make driving the rented Ford a chore; still, she could have managed the trip. No, it was simply that on certain nights she wished to remain on the hill, to absorb the starlit atmosphere and to deepen her feel for the spaces she would soon call home. Too, her mention to the priest of her financial straits made her resist charging another meal in town. She recalled she had a third of a loaf of day-old sourdough in the cupboard here. Maybe half a jar of honey. That would do for dinner. The bills were accumulating: the car, the room on the plaza, the hut repairs. And now the doctor. She needed to expedite the work schedule, to energize Ramon and Matías, her two-man construction crew—they had vanished six days ago, promising to reappear at week's end, muttering something about a cousin's wedding in Taos. The day before that, they had wasted most of their sunlight hours arguing over knotholed lumber. ("Matías, he choose bad boards!" Ramon yelled at his partner between frequent sandwich breaks.) They accused each other of measuring the *vigas* too short.

While she cleaned the teacups, Elsie wondered again what the editors at *Harper's* were up to, back in New York. They could ease her money woes if they'd stop hesitating and finally accept her proposal to write a series of articles about a woman's adventures in the West, restoring an ancient Mexican adobe.

With difficulty, she unrolled the orange-and-gray wool blanket and pulled a cotton pillow from a pinewood pantry next to her bookshelf. Willa's peacock feather brightened the place. Elsie lighted two stubby candles and set them on the floor beside the pallet. The flames hopped; shadows dimpled the yellow glow on the walls like mild rain stirring a pond's surface. The light pulled the walls close. The match's sulfurous after-scent filled the space, deepening the cozy comfort. From Elsie's window moonlight, silvering blue rabbit brush, swelled her perceptions: it was as if her bones relaxed, along with the fabric of her skin. Then a shrinking sensation, a feeling of being enclosed—not unpleasantly—by adobe, plaster, wood. She imagined herself an exotic product wrapped on a shelf: *Woman from the East. Price slashed. Note the bandage. Damaged goods.* Certainly, this was how Father Courvaille saw her: a misdelivered package, a privileged dilettante impaired by her ignorance, landing where she didn't belong. If *Harper's* did accept her pieces, would that confirm the priest's impression of her? Elsie Sergeant: an oblivious tourist exploiting locals for money? What would Willa say?

Months ago, when Elsie first arrived in Santa Fe, Willa had mailed her a volume "for company on those long, arid nights when you're exhausted from your labors but too sore to sleep": Gauguin's *The Tahitian Journals.* How like Willa! Thoughtful, of course. But sardonic, as well. *Pugilistic* was Elsie's word for it. Gauguin was not, by any means, Willa's favorite painter. His work was too crude. But she had defended his vision one afternoon at her New York apartment, a few years before the threat of the war, when Elsie had returned from a Paris sojourn praising her discovery of the Cubists: "It's fascinating, the way they present multiple perspectives on the canvas." She had even confessed to Willa that, one night, she'd nearly succumbed to the charms of a young Cubist, an olive-skinned man with garlic on his breath. Drunkenly, he had asked her to dance as five or six violins soared to a disharmonious climax in a Left Bank bistro. The story appalled Willa—the screech of the music, the impulsive, booze-soaked seduction. Elsie saw in her friend's troubled eyes exactly how she imagined the scene, nothing at all like the sweet, honest truth of it. Willa's Paris was the stone-girded classicism of the bridges above the Seine, not the pissed-on alley cobbles so enchanting to Elsie. And of course, Willa deplored the Cubists. "Sloppiness and confusion," she said. "Junk theories of art! If you want something *truly* revolutionary, how about Puvis de Chavannes? His frescoes of Saint Geneviève?" Elsie didn't know what she was talking about. "Monumental and static. Legendary. Not like this fashion for scraps!" She disguised her aesthetic revulsion as concern for Elsie's innocence, but Elsie understood her response as a renewal of their fight: Tradition ("the *old* modernism") versus Reform. In the eyes of her friend, Elsie was susceptible to novelty, to the adolescent thrill of smashing everything valuable. It was in this context that Willa had mentioned Gauguin: "A primitive, to be sure, but at least he seeks the pure essence of experience—life's simple, unchangeable basics."

Now, in her candlelit hut, leaning tiredly on her power stick, Elsie smiled at the painter's journals. Willa would never cease trying to score points, tightening her grip on what she hoped was her protégé's malleable imagination. Well. Perhaps the book *would* be entertaining.

She propped her cane against the wall and lowered herself to her pallet. A horrid curl of *something* slithered beneath the larder curtain. Her heartbeat quickened. She jumped for her cane, thudding her foot against a chair leg. Swearing under her breath, she swept the stick back and forth beneath the curtain fringe. Nothing. Where did it go? She knelt, disregarding the throb in her ankle, ruffling her blanket, searching each corner of her pallet. How could a snake get into the house? Silly question. What would keep it out? For the next half hour she stuffed rags into wall crannies where a creature might enter. Tomorrow, she must stir up a bucket of fresh adobe mud. Plug the gaps.

She picked up her book, watching for shadows. Startling: a coyote call from below, from deep in the ocean-green wash. Months ago, before she'd left New York to catch the train out west, a young intern in the *Harper's* offices had lent her a copy of a short story, "To Build a Fire," by a young writer named Jack London. "You might find it of interest," said the intern, "since you'll soon be stomping through wilderness." Elsie hadn't liked the piece, its tight, blocky prose, so inelegant compared to, say, Willa's lush austerity—"primitive," just like your man Gauguin, Willa would say—but its lingering power returned to her now as she trembled on the hut's cold floor, the anxiety of the character running out of time, losing hope, as fierce howling closed in around him . . .

She chose a random page of the painter's journals: "Everyone may create romance at the will of his imagination, and at a glance have his soul invaded by the most profound memories," Gauguin wrote.

Elsie pulled the candles closer. She turned another page: "It was Europe, the Europe which I had thought to shake off by coming to the island, but here I have encountered repeatedly the aggravating circumstances of colonial snobbism, and the imitation, grotesque even to the point of caricature, of our customs, fashions, vices, and absurdities of civilization. Was I to have made this far journey, only to find the very thing which I had fled?"

She closed the book and dropped it in her lap. She heard, again, Father Courvaille: *humanity's sins . . . the world's sadness.*

Naturally, fleeing home never eased anyone's burdens, Elsie thought. The world was the world, and we remained the same, wherever we went. I could have taught Mr. Gauguin *that* bitter lesson. Here she was, lying in the near dark, trying to ignore her injured foot and reading a book from Willa—a melancholy repeat of her situation four years ago, languishing in the American Hospital on the outskirts of Paris. All it took was one terrible morning—one morning when humanity's sins disguised themselves as a German prayer missal, a benign-looking booby trap in a small, marshy meadow.

As Elsie sank, that day, into the stinking marl, tasting blood— shrapnel had hammered her face and arms as well as her legs and feet—her first thought was: *Willa would say, "I told you so."*

Then she gagged on the odor of feces and steaming gristle that had been the woman chatting beside her.

Months before, when *The New Republic* had assigned Elsie (at her request) to become a war correspondent, stationed in her dear, beleaguered France just behind the front lines, she had promised Willa she would take no risks. She had believed the world she loved to be immortal. In spite of grave dangers, surely it would be a simple matter to find refuge in a red-roofed cottage somewhere in a ripe green valley, or in the city among genial men assuring their comrades, smugly, as if it were a joke, the only thing they could be certain of was that nothing was ever certain. But upon arrival, on one of those gray and slimy afternoons in Paris in midwinter, she'd discovered that the front lines were hard to determine. Economic deprivation had created bread queues and clothing shortages and the closing of bookshops all along the river. Hawkers hustled whatever books remained from wooden street carts as if they were neckties or shoes. Obituaries bloated the newspapers. Life's smallest activities seemed the equivalent of a burial.

Escorted by military personnel to a temporary command post just outside the city, she entered a hornet's nest of confusion. Heavy equipment moved incomprehensibly through marshes and mud. Then one morning, walking through a clover field, she stepped on what she took to be a cow's liver. A young lieutenant informed her she had stumbled upon a day-old mass of dark, coagulated blood. She stood by a barbed-wire fence as medics rushed into the field, patiently rounded up the remains of a soldier, and pieced him together on a stretcher. That very afternoon in a train depot, recently the site of a bombing, she tripped on a stringy, gelatinous clump—like a salty sea creature covered with flies. Intensely studying the object, she found herself staring at a man's severed wrist.

One morning before dawn a jaunty lieutenant escorted her and another reporter off the train at Epernay and drove them to Rheims and into the Marne to inspect a battle's aftermath. The day broke misty and cool but mildly pleasant, dew-soft and quiet with a promise of rising temperatures late in the afternoon. He warned them not to touch anything on the ground—even the most familiar-looking articles, wallets, shoes, spectacles, and rings, might not be what they seemed—but Elsie's companion was an irrepressible enthusiast.

At the moment of impact, Elsie felt herself swell to an enormous size under agonizing pressure. A short while later, as she catapulted in and out of consciousness, she perceived great, flapping wings resolving into men's faces—gaunt faces, like insane ascetics in a Goya etching. They babbled in English and French. Someone told her they were going to build a house around her leg. Somehow, she grasped what this meant: medics would try to apply a splint. She was bundled onto a scratchy stretcher, awaiting the field ambulance that would rush her to a hospital. With a damp cloth a young man tried to wash her face. "No, no!" she screamed at him, flailing as if to stave off bees.

Water, water. Next she knew, she was gazing through the dim blue light of a hospital ward at a thin, reddened face considerably shot to pieces, a mass of ribbons: an Oklahoma boy piled into a nearby bed. He would not last the month. The walls smelled noxious. A gray official, incongruously dressed in a wrinkled white tuxedo, passed among the infirm offering each patient the condolences of the French government. A male nurse gave her sickish tea embittered with green lemon. Through a clear plastic tube, cold, stinging liquid trickled into her left foot. As far as she could see, she was the lone woman in a room of anguished men.

She dreamed that night of thousands of wounded soldiers ripping off their poultices, choosing to bleed to death in a bid to end all wars. She woke angered at the world's patience: *Why do we* tolerate *such carnage?* Squadrons of bombers throbbed overhead, rattling the hospital's grimy windows.

In the next several weeks—no telephones or cabling capacity—she wrote letters and tried to take notes for the magazine. She admitted, in a card to Willa, that what she once took to be moral courage was only the strength of her two good legs: as long as she believed she could outrun any challenge, she was heedless, cavalier. Helpless now, she knew herself to be a coward, an impotent, aching creature.

Gazing at her cast, she realized the doctors had treated her wounds as if she were a soldier—that is, as if her body were that of a young man. *So this is what it's like,* she thought. How much did the body really matter? Was it dangerous to think this way—especially if the body was all there was?

One late afternoon, she asked an exhausted nurse how he could make his rounds so uncomplainingly in this dispiriting place. A sad, tired grin. "Madame, les blessés sont plus intéressants que lest morts," he said: *The wounded are more interesting than the dead.*

Willa's new book arrived on a cloudy morning when Elsie felt more physically spry but weaker of heart after such lengthy confinement to bed. Along with an advance copy of *My Ántonia,* Willa had included in her package several recent issues of American magazines and a short note of concern, urging Elsie to hurry on back to the States so Willa could nurture her.

"All the years that have passed have not dimmed my memory of that first glorious autumn. The new country lay open before me: there were no fences in those days, and I could choose my own way over the grass uplands, trusting the pony to get me home again," Elsie read in Willa's novel. Willa's Western voice. Her *true* voice.

Elsie smiled and shut her eyes, imagining her friend striding across alfalfa fields, caring not a whit if the hem of her calico skirt blackened with sheep manure. Somehow with this book, even more than with *The Song of the Lark,* Willa had summoned the courage to cast off the stuffy literary conventions she had learned working as a magazine editor in New York. Here, she channeled the plain speech of her prairie upbringing, the whisper of wind in the wheat. She had found the rhythms of unseen critters skittering in the rafters of a barn! Elsie wondered if *she* would ever be brave enough to explore the roots of *her* earliest language and try her hand at writing a novel.

She remembered her friend's first slim book, the awkward story of an engineer—inspired by a bridge Willa used to pass in Boston on her way to the house she loved so much on Charles Street. That novel was a misfire: grand, rolling sentences bound by the nasal cadences of privileged Easterners—the "very best" people in "sophisticated" settings. Willa was not a New Englander. She should never have tried to be Henry James. But James had been a hero of hers in those days, the toast of Charles Street.

For decades (Willa had explained to Elsie), the lady of the Charles Street house, Annie Fields, widow of the *Atlantic*'s editor, had entertained an international literary elite in the second-floor library. "I was born too late," Willa lamented, "missing those days of splendor when Hawthorne, James, and Emerson traded quips with Mrs. Fields over glasses of sherry and Shakespearian folios purchased by her husband in London." Later, after her husband's death, Mrs. Fields invited Sarah Orne Jewett, a writer known for her quaint New England sketches, to occupy the house with her. The women ornamented the drafty rooms like a pair of bejeweled lions. While living in Boston on assignment for *McClure's* magazine, Willa met them through mutual friends. Almost immediately, Miss Jewett recognized the depth of Willa's literary sensibility. She encouraged her to quit the magazine world, to devote herself to novel writing full time, to marshal, guard, and mature her natural forces. "Find your quiet center," she said. She ushered Willa into the dark mahogany hallways, made her feel at home among the poets of the past. On Elsie's one visit to Boston, for a meeting with Willa, Miss Jewett, and Mrs. Fields over a pot of English tea, Elsie sensed Willa squelching her excessive energy to avoid damaging the ladies' delicate furnishings. Similarly, the snuffing of her best instincts undermined that first novel.

Of course, Elsie could never tell Willa that. Willa was her elder by eight years, certainly more experienced in publishing and writing. From the first, she had seen herself as Elsie's mentor, wiser and calmer. "Hm. Well, I suppose pamphleteering has its place," she'd said with a pert sniff, in her musty editorial office at *McClure's* on West 23rd Street, the day Elsie had trundled in, wrapped in her cheap Paris cloak, to discuss the article she'd submitted to the magazine. It was a five-thousand-word piece on the squalor of tenement life on the Lower East Side. "You don't want to be a muckraker, do you?" Willa said. "You look like a Jamesian to me. Yes?"

Elsie had nearly cried, convinced she was being dismissed. Willa asked her where she'd gone to school. "Bryn Mawr? Oh Lord," Willa said. She loomed over Elsie, wearing a brightly striped blouse and an Irish tweed skirt. "Every journalist I've ever met who was trained on that campus has found the world wanting and has taken it upon herself to rewrite the planet's rules so we'll all live happily ever after!"

"But surely you don't want babies to die!" Elsie exploded. Her cloak slipped to the floor.

"What on Earth are you talking about?"

"Infants! Sickened by the odors of outdoor privies, dirty pigtails cooked on open stoves—"

"Pigtails?" Willa interjected. "*Cooked*? Dear girl, I don't have the faintest idea what you're—"

Exasperated, Elsie said, "You didn't even *read* my piece, did you?" She pointed to one of the pages. "Pigtails! They cut them off the heads of Chinese criminals. It's big business."

"*Who*?"

"Wigmakers! I explain it right here! Page three! They weave the hair into rats for Gibson girls to wear under their pompadours. And what about this?" She pulled another page from the manuscript. "Here. Italian families just off the boats. Every day—I describe it in great detail—they're subjected to—"

"Yes, yes, I know those Italians," Willa said dryly. "I used to live in Washington Place, next to the Italian Quarter. Their noisy children would splash in the fountains on hot summer evenings, beneath endless flocks of defecating pigeons."

Elsie shrugged, retrieved her wrap, and rose to leave.

"Sit down, Miss Sergeant," Willa commanded her. "No need to get hysterical. The tone of your article is not altogether infelicitous."

Ten years later, hidden away in the American Hospital—like a busted stove from one of the tenement rooms she'd described—Elsie marveled at the lyrical tone of Willa's Nebraska novel. Willa had freed herself from James's convoluted sentences. Since suffering her injury, nothing had made Elsie more homesick than *My Ántonia*, though she'd never traveled west of Massachusetts. She longed to see the America Willa praised: an old plough in the glare of the sun. Or even *more* remote: "I think you would love New Mexico's mesas and golden plateaus," Willa told Elsie one day. They were lunching together in Madison Square Park after an editorial meeting over another of Elsie's pieces. "I just returned from visiting my brother out there—he works for the railroads," Willa said. "My dear, in the far West, there are boulders shaped like giant camels, and lovely Mexican boys singing dance tunes that will lift you, spinning, into the air!"

Recalling all this now—reliving the hospital experience from her hut in Tesuque—Elsie wondered what *artistry* required, over and above the monthly deadlines of ad hoc journalism. For all of Willa's blind spots—and her novel of war would be riddled with them, Elsie thought—she had committed herself solely to her art. An admirable enterprise, though a lonely one. (Willa had once told Elsie she wished to be nothing more than a fountain pen, a conduit for the unfettered flow of ink.)

A hot pulse seized Elsie's foot and she bolted upright, spilling the book to the floor. It fell open on the reproduction of a painting made in the Marquesas Islands—two bare-breasted women, "Tahitian Eves," Gauguin had called them, "very subtle, very knowing in their naivety, and utterly without shame." *Romantic nonsense*, Elsie thought. *The aesthetic elevation of the 'primitive' to the sacred.* Then she caught herself. Wasn't this precisely how Father Courvaille saw *her*?

She massaged her instep through the bandage. A chilly gray blur. Something unfurled by the larder. The movement froze her. A snake, all right—what sort she couldn't tell. Not a very large one. Still, she wouldn't sleep tonight until she got it out of here. She scrabbled for her cane. Hopping, she approached the larder curtain, flung it back, and saw the creature disappear down a hole about the width of a shin bone. With the cane she moved a bag of flour over the crack. She bolstered the bag with a pair of heavy boots. Exhausted, she staggered back against the wall, her foot burning beneath the sticky wrapping. Down the hill, a wild dog moaned at the moon.

3

Since the war, the morning mirror had not treated her kindly. Her face had always been thin, with a long aquiline nose. In low lighting, her dark, deep-set eyes could appear tubercular, while her slender lips resembled nothing so much as an "equals" sign in a mathematical equation. It had never been a face to inspire respect or even much notice at all. But now the nicks from the shrapnel, puckered pink, like erratic lines in a child's connect-the-dots game, gave her a perforated look, strengthening the impression that she lacked any depth that might prompt further inspection. Certainly, Ramon and Matías did not take seriously her stern stares nor did they follow her slightest commands.

Tying back her hair with a fat cotton braid, she recalled the time Willa had scratched her own scalp with a hairpin and developed a blood infection. This was several years ago, before the war. She had spent three weeks in a hospital with the back of her head shaved. What Elsie recalled most vividly about the incident was Willa's refusal to feel sorry for herself. She quoted her friend Olive Fremstad, the New York opera singer on whom she had based much of *The Song of the Lark*: "If it had been a railroad wreck one might endure it; but when it's a pin scratch, it's simply silly." The disturbing side of Willa's stoicism revealed itself as impatience—"People who go and have grotesque accidents are clowns," Willa said. She was witheringly intolerant of the wounded. One day she told Elsie, "People minus their leg or their hair are roaringly funny and ought to be laughed at and exhibited, not coddled." Elsie understood that her friend's cruel bravado covered an unspeakable terror of weakness; she forgave Willa's callousness. But following the accident in the Marne, she believed Willa never again regarded her with whole-hearted compassion. Always, a slight recoil, even a trace of contempt, shivered through Willa's shoulders whenever she spoke to Elsie. Reminders of mortality had no place in Willa's ordered world.

And now the men who would complete her hut, if they ever returned, failed to honor her; they glanced at her scars, emboldened by her vulnerability (over and above the fact that she was a woman): predators sensing the end of the hunt, the prey's faltering steps.

She boiled water for coffee over the firepit, where she'd sat with Father Courvaille. Then she mixed mud in a bucket to prevent midnight reptiles from getting into the house.

Around noon, as she was preparing to calcimine a sunny portion of the dining room wall, she heard the clattering and burping of a truck down the hill. *Milagro!* Ramon and Matías spilled from the dusty cab, slow and stumbling, still hungover, it appeared, from the wedding festivities. They had not yet noticed her; she stood at the lip of the hill observing their lanky, disheveled frames against the backdrop of the old Tesuque schoolhouse. Beyond the canyon stood the shuttered former train depot, blurred by heat waves, small as a matchbox from this perspective. The purple shadows in the seams of the Jemez Mountains brought the pink foothills into startling relief—almost a physical strain on the retina. Rich, forest-green fields sloped south toward Santa Fe, invisible past the yellow horizon, hazed with pollen. High, salmon-hued clouds, ridged like fish scales, sped west as swiftly as a river over ranches, dice-like and flat. Near the Arroyo Seco, nestled among sugar-white hills, villages lined up like wooden dominoes.

Ramon tripped on an enormous rose of Castile, in full yellow bloom. Matías offered him a hand up. In spite of their slapstick movements, the men exhibited a sulky self-consciousness—like adolescents testing adult gestures. Perhaps the formal demeanor Elsie had adopted with them, to impress on them the seriousness of their work together, was having some effect after all. "Welcome back," she called. They straightened and waved. Then: "He is *hurt!*"

cried Ramon, pointing at her bandages. He had never distinguished masculine from feminine pronouns in English, despite her attempts to teach him.

"I took a fall," she said calmly, "but it won't keep me from my labors, and I certainly don't want to slow the two of you down." They shouted concern. This irritated her. She recognized the hollowness of their sympathy, an effort to curry her favor—she had tried similar tactics with New York editors. (They never worked.) She assured the men that Dr. Gonzalez had taken good care of her.

"Gonzalez?" Matías said. "He is a hero."

"Well, no. My injury wasn't *that* bad. It was just—"

"He has fought the Indians for many years now."

"Oh. You mean his fence? The land around his house?"

"That land belongs to the Mexicans. The Indians want to steal it back from us."

Elsie laughed. As on many occasions, she was struck by the ancient contradictions of this place: the way the Americans, the Spanish, the Mestizos, and the Pueblos differed in color and outlook, in psychological substance, and yet remained tightly fused, like rock strata on the Pajarito Plateau.

She said, "Well, matters are a bit messier than—"

"*Matters?*" Matías spat. "Ours is ours." He gazed at her wound—rather meanly, Elsie thought. "You are not on *their* side?"

She'd had trouble enough with her workers without engaging in an abstract and unwinnable political skirmish. Reluctantly, she backed down. "Of course not. Now, I've got to hang some butter down the well, and in the meantime, if you two could get the gypsum, pull the cheesecloth from the ceiling beams, and start whitewashing the living room."

After storing the butter, she scooped mud from the acequia floodplain. She gathered the gold-lacquer screens and Japanese prints (butterflies, plum blossoms, bamboo bridges) that would decorate her bedroom, along with tin candelabra and cherry bureaus; these she moved to the center of the room, away from freshly plastered walls where, as the afternoon temperatures spiked, mud still fell in thick cakes.

Matías unrolled a bundle of ashfelt roofing in a hardscrabble patch she hoped to turn into a garden someday. From a sweaty leather bag Ramon emptied a batch of number 9 nails. He'd hauled them in the truck from Santa Fe. Elsie's ankle burned but she attempted to ignore the pain. Twice, she tripped on her cane. The sun was big and vermilion in the west when she overheard Matías chattering with Ramon outside her dining room window. Her Spanish was poor but she caught the gist: *Needs a good, hard man to boss her.*

She hobbled through the front portal, turned, and appraised her hut. It was the sort of house a child might draw: simple squares unevenly spaced, everything at a tilt. Nevertheless, she felt satisfied. She fantasized building a series of steps, seven perhaps, like the stoop of the Charles Street house—a gentle elevation as you entered the hut, announcing your arrival at a "sacred space." (Willa, a devoted reader of *The Divine Comedy*, always referred to Charles Street in hushed, heavenly tones.)

The beehive oven, a tumbledown affair crowning the ridge just south of the kitchen, remained to be built; behind the house, she'd forgotten to save room for a terrace. Tomorrow, she'd remeasure. Overall, she thought, a pretty good day's work.

She went that night into Santa Fe. She parked the rented Ford in a gravel lot behind the Capital Pharmacy, the back room of which doubled as a real estate office. A month ago, she'd signed the deed to her hut there. She shuffled across the plaza, tap-tapping her cane, to the Wasiolek Manor Hotel, where she kept a room. The restaurant just off the south end of the lobby smelled of custard, warm sugar, and lemon. A hint of peaty malt liquor. Affixed to the walls, carriage-house lanterns—like items salvaged from Boston house demolitions years ago. They contributed to the lobby's venerable atmosphere. Rich, buttery light swept across deep green wallpaper. Maroon velvet curtains soaked up sparkles from the ceiling's chandeliers. In spite of the hotel's efforts to duplicate Eastern sophistication, the imported styles produced the opposite effect, reinforcing Western rawness, the conviction that history had a long way to go here yet.

In the restaurant entryway she ran into Margretta Stewart and Martha and Elizabeth White, the three Bryn Mawr ladies who had preceded her to New Mexico, purchased property, and renovated old adobes. They had inserted themselves into local life, hoping (they said) to shape America's future in communities whose political infrastructure was still young, still evolving—all in the activist Bryn Mawr tradition.

Elsie liked the women, but since arriving she'd kept herself apart from them, from a need to continue her long recuperation after the war. Self-protection: surely she'd learned *this* tactic from Willa. In turn, the ladies remained rather cool to her, if friendly enough. It was up to her to make conciliatory gestures, and she would, she would, as soon as she finished her hut . . .

They all wore high-buckled riding boots, khaki pants, and thick white cotton shirts. Turquoise stones swung on silver chains around their necks. The casual clothing emphasized the stiffness of their movements. No one here would mistake them for natives of this place. They cooed over Elsie's foot. Her leg, wrapped in discolored bandages, looked like a burnt log. "Oh, my dear!" said Elizabeth. "I feel for you, truly I do, working with these local Mexicans. We all have their best interests at heart . . . they've never been properly compensated for the jobs they do . . . still, they *have* adopted certain unfortunate habits, haven't they?"

"Yes," Margretta said. "You *must* keep an eye on them. It's a sad fact, a failing of the larger culture. The better you treat them, the more they'll take advantage of you."

"Will we see you at the Corn Dance?" asked Martha.

Elsie had heard of this desert ritual, to be enacted at the Tesuque Pueblo at month's end, but she didn't know the outsider etiquette. "Are we allowed?" she said.

"Oh yes. You can't bring photographic equipment or notebooks—none of the implements of your trade, I'm afraid—but *we'll* certainly be welcomed, especially given our well-known and vocal support for the Pueblos' way of life."

"We've been very active since settling here," Elizabeth added.

"I'm sure," Elsie said.

"Do come." Martha touched her arm. "We'll bring parasols and blankets and a picnic luncheon."

"Perhaps I'll see you there." Not likely, Elsie thought. Self-invited. Smug. None of this felt right to her.

"Splendid," Martha said. The ladies "toodled" off.

Elsie asked a porter to take her war-battered bag to her room. She seated herself in the restaurant near a big stone fireplace. She'd brought *The Tahitian Journals*; a light meal, a glass of wine, a little reading, and then she'd treat herself to a warm bath. (Somehow, she'd have to get these bandages changed in a day or two.) Finally, a soft bed before returning tomorrow to another hard day at the hut.

For one night, she'd not worry about money.

She realized this was the same table she'd occupied a week ago when Mountain Lake joined her. A strange chance meeting, catching her utterly by surprise. "Elasticity is a property of time," he'd said to her, again and again, as if she were a child unable to grasp his simple concepts.

His real name was Ochwiay Bianco. Roughly, this translated as "Mountain Lake," he told her. He was a former chief of the Taos Pueblos, a man of forty or fifty—it was hard to tell and he didn't know. Elsie had encountered him early in the afternoon on the plaza near the hotel. At first, she had thought he was playing a role for her benefit. His taciturnity matched her image, gleaned from press reports, of a Native Elder. He said he had walked to town to observe the "Europeans." Many days had passed since he'd mingled body and spirit with figures outside his family circle. From season to season, it was necessary to reacquaint oneself with the rhythms of others, he said, to detect imbalances on the surface of the Earth that might require correction.

Elsie had to admit, with her limited knowledge of Native cultures, she was not in a position to determine what was and wasn't "authentic."

On impulse, she invited him to lunch. He had never been inside the hotel—indeed, he had not entered *any* of the buildings on the plaza. Over green salads and corn on the cob he tried, at her request, to illustrate his meaning of "balance." (Already, she imagined introducing him to Dr. Jung.) Time was fluid, he said. It could dry to a trickle or swell to a flood. Calendars and clocks—these were mental dams, but they could not hold time's essence. The Earth was like a hut. "The Pueblos . . . we are a people who live on the roof of the world," Mountain Lake explained. "We are the sons of the Father Sun. We help our father go across the sky." As he spoke, his handsome face remained as still as a mask—stiff, striated.

Elsie thought, *Yes, yes, Dr. Jung* must *meet him*! Her hunch had been right. The men had much in common, including a reverence for Nature and the Mind, and she recognized many links between them. Elsie was convinced they'd learn from each other—an enriching exchange. How could she impress upon Mountain Lake the time and date of Dr. Jung's arrival? The old chief didn't reckon hours the way "Europeans" did.

"I will be here," he said. "I will know."

"How?"

"I will be here," he repeated, nodding at the plaza. If this was a performance, it was remarkably convincing.

She wondered where he was tonight and if she'd really see him again. The stares she caught now from adjacent tables reminded her of the looks she got that day sitting with the chief. It was clear her fellow diners didn't approve of her; she'd had the temerity to parade her injury into their playground, disturbing the night's elegance and their illusions of unending good health. She ignored them and ordered a glass of Chardonnay. She opened Gauguin: "It is the rare master who can have anything he wants, yet who scorns decorations, honors, fortune, without bitterness, without jealousies," she read.

"I don't care if the Republican candidate turns out to be Satan, I'll vote for him anyway," roared a man at the table to her left. He wore a black tie and waved a clumpy cigar as long as a beat cop's billy club.

"All I know is, the secretary of the interior is plenty worried," said one of his dinner mates, also finely dressed. "I spoke to him last week in Washington." Two women in pearls and white gowns sat with the men. Conspicuously, the ladies refused to acknowledge Elsie's presence. Their disgust with her was even more apparent than if they'd stood gaping at her leg.

"The elections will provide a midcourse correction. Besides, Senator Bursum has matters well in hand. There won't *be* any land disputes once he's finished." The man relighted the tip of his cheroot. "Once you tell the Indians they have to go to *court* . . . well, that's the last you'll see of them."

"True enough. Holm'll fix their wagons for them."

Freeloaders, Elsie mused. Men like this ruled the West now, political pawnbrokers selling off what the pioneers had procured. This new breed of men, blowing smoke in the banks, the law offices, and the courts, packing juries, and padding the pockets of congressmen, never risked anything, she thought. They had simply inherited the game, and now they'd set about realigning the playing board so they—the fawning bishops and the knights—could move any way they wanted, serving their senile kings.

Elsie chuckled quietly—drawing stern looks—surprised at the overheated rhetoric in her head. Her passion for the West. Surely a gift from Willa, just like the book in her lap.

She remembered sitting with Willa over breakfast in Delmonico's one morning, watching her seethe at a pair of New York businessmen. While buttering their toast they debated "cheap farm shares." "I could snap up all of Nebraska for a pittance right now," said one of the men, laughing, and Willa nearly reached across the table to slap him. Elsie loved her friend in that moment. The slums on the Lower East Side didn't stir her sense of injustice, but mutter one discouraging word about the Great American Plains, and you'd unleash her ire.

Willa had invited Elsie to breakfast that morning to ask about her war traumas. Elsie had just returned to the States after weeks in the hospital in Paris. With a steel cane she limped past indifferent strollers on the sidewalks. She got the impression Willa disdained her for stepping into an accident. Willa's chin hardened and she thrust her shoulders forward. She smiled softly—a gesture meant to be disarming—and said, "You know, the body was intended to remain as God made it." She cracked bitter jokes about her scalp wound. "Ever since, I've been forced to buy the most *expensive* hats! That thin patch of hair on the back of my head has never fully grown back." That morning, she wore what appeared to be a velvet turban trimmed with silver lace. It might have been a prop from an opera stage. It nearly extinguished the intent face beneath it.

And yet it was *Elsie's* wound that absorbed Willa. "Can you speak of it? I want to know."

This was not a friend offering sympathy. Rather, here was a writer nosing around for research purposes. Willa seemed possessed, with an eye in every pore. She had heard of "shell shock." "What is it, exactly?" she said. "How does it manifest itself?" Elsie started to speak of "nervous cases," the remarkable advances being made in psychological studies by the likes of Drs. Freud and Jung, but Willa would have none of it. "This Viennese poseur, why is everybody reading him?" she said. "Tolstoy knew much more about the human mind than he does—with no *isms* attached. But tell me, tell me the story of the war."

And that was the trouble, Elsie thought. For Willa, war was simply a story. It was not lived experience.

They walked together to Central Park, Willa oblivious to Elsie's struggles with the cane. She prattled about the "perishing" New

York summers, how someday she might like to purchase a get-away cottage—off the coast of New Brunswick, perhaps, Grand Manan . . . "Of course, it's just a fantasy. I'd have to sell a lot more books to afford it . . ."

Elsie loved her friend's belling voice, even as she tuned it out until it was merely music. She loved the burnt-coffee smell of the heavy urban air and the faint moan of ferryboats along the Hudson. Her Northeastern upbringing had jaded her early, made her too keenly aware of the city's provincialism, its pretensions, but my god she *had* been homesick for it all! Still, a whiff of melancholy seemed to rise like steam from the avenue grates; the shoppers' shoulders hunched—a hangover from the war, Elsie supposed. Or perhaps she had hauled this sadness home with her and projected it onto her fellows. (What would Dr. Freud say?)

But Willa—apparently, Willa experienced an entirely different world. Up and down Broadway, in restaurants and hotels, every-where you looked, she said, you saw "one of ours"—this was her phrase for the humble doughboys who had (in Willa's estimation) "won the war for us" and who hid their Purple Hearts beneath their greatcoats, in true heroic fashion. "They're all so surprisingly endearing and vital!" she exclaimed. Elsie knew then that her friend, once distraught over the prospect of conflict, had somehow ide-alized the tragedy in Europe. She also suspected war would figure in Willa's next novel.

Willa confirmed this once they had taken a seat in the park at a skimpy iron table in the trellised old tea house. Violet wisteria festooned the glass peaks on the roof's main slope. The tea house was one of Willa's favorite spots in the city. It seemed to belong to the Victorian era: a lighthouse keeper's residence, magically spirited here to the park.

The red fur in Willa's coat glowed hotly against the flowers, clus-tered in cool purple bunches behind the tables.

She told Elsie she had received a telegram informing her that a cousin of hers from Nebraska, a boy named G. P. Cather, had been killed in the battle of Cantigny. "I'm moved to tell the story of his life," she said. "I feel it as a duty."

"I see. You must have loved him very much," Elsie said.

"Not at all. I couldn't stand him, actually. He was a bully. And he was intellectually backward. He had no interest in the world beyond the feeding of the pigs on his father's farm. But the telegram said he died protecting the men in his unit. He fought with valor and courage. So here is this stunted Nebraska kid, always butting his way through life—he seems to have found his true self, his best self, in the army, in the rigors of warfare. This has all the makings of a great American story, don't you think?"

Elsie felt a chill: Willa's thinking was dangerous and naive. Elsie knew better than to argue with her friend, but she was determined to say nothing more of her own experiences in France, details that might enhance Willa's misguided ideas of glorifying violence. The newspapers were already full of such careless bunk.

Later, Elsie remained largely silent as they meandered down Greenwich Street. The day had got on; Willa insisted on making lunch. They would stop at the Jefferson Street Market for apples and grapes and Camembert cheese. Willa said she planned to begin her new novel in the Charles Street house in Boston. She was going to stay with Mrs. Fields. Mrs. Fields was terribly lonely ever since Miss Jewett had died. "I'll never forget one of Miss Jewett's last pieces of advice to me," Willa told Elsie. "She pulled me close to her bed and said, 'You must know the world before you can know the village!'"

Near the market, on the corner of West 11th and Seventh Avenue, they heard someone playing an out-of-tune piano through an open fifth-floor window in a square and undistinguished brownstone: Bach's "Sheep May Safely Graze." Willa's face grew soft. Her eyes misted. "Ah," she said. "Whenever life becomes overwhelming and it seems as though there is nothing to look forward to but death and despair . . ." (Elsie had never heard her speak this way) "Bach's steadiness makes you feel everything will be well!"

"To the Republicans!"

"To Senator Bursum!"

The table next to Elsie erupted in a second round of drinks. The ladies glowered at her. She ordered another glass of wine and, still flush with memories of her day with Willa, a plate of bread and some Camembert cheese.

Within the half hour, the group rose to leave. At that moment, another gaggle attacked the room, including Father Courvaille, dressed not in his clerical garb but in a shabby gray suit. No tie. He was clearly inebriated. He kept wrapping his hammy arms around a loud, laughing woman who wore an orange wool coat too thick for the weather. Elsie averted her gaze.

She finished her cheese. The priest caught her eye. His face was alarmingly florid. He waved and then he approached her table, dipping and weaving, favoring his gouty foot. "Will you join us?" he asked.

"Thank you, no. I have a long day tomorrow."

"Reshaping our hills to suit your fine tastes?"

She ignored his sarcasm and returned some of her own. "A parishioner?" she said, nodding at the woman standing half-in, half-out of the coat.

"Bonnie. The mother of my children."

Elsie blinked.

"You disapprove?" said the priest.

"It's just that . . . I didn't think . . ."

"Yes. And Rome would agree with you. But we are a long way from Rome here. That's what I was trying to tell you the other day. I know my people."

"I guess you do."

"They wouldn't accept a spiritual leader who wasn't one of theirs. But *pah*! Here I am, preaching at you again. Come, let me buy you a drink."

"No, no."

He watched her face, the way he might study a page of his breviary. "If you want to settle here, Miss Sergeant, you should really get to know folks," he said. "Have you heard of the Corn Dance?"

"In fact, I was talking about it earlier tonight."

"Come to the Pueblo at the end of the month. Observe the celebration. Let me introduce you to people. Show you around."

Was it merely serendipity that she had received two invitations to the ritual in the space of two hours? What would Jung say?

"Freddy!" called the woman in the coat.

Elsie smiled at the man. "*Freddy?*"

He mock bowed. "At your service. Think about the dance."

"I will."

The Tesuque Pueblo nestled among great box-elder trees planted along sandy roads puddled here and there with muddy holes attractive to gnats and flies. A bit farther on, by the banks of the Little Tesuque River, pink cottonwood blossoms waved like candle flames in the breeze. The kiva and the whitewashed church stood against a mountain tinted the enameled blue of a Chinese teacup. It was named for a local watermelon.

Elsie stepped with her cane into an alleyway just off the plaza to avoid a parade of figures on horseback, the tops of their heads bound in bright red handkerchiefs. The horses moved with slow dignity in swelling clouds of dust. Covered wagons followed them, shaped like giant sausage links. Glare from sun-bleached adobe walls forced people gathered in the plaza to shield their eyes.

The sweet smell of fruit on the wind was nearly maddening.

As promised, Martha, Margretta, and Elizabeth had arrived in their high-buckled boots bearing blankets and baskets of food. They set up their sun umbrellas on a hillock by the church. They greeted Elsie warmly. A squat brown woman passed behind them, silent, eyes cast to the ground. On her head she balanced a clay water jar. Her single-piece garment, corn-tassel green, silver buttons shining like fireflies, drew admiring "oohs" from Elizabeth. She pressed the woman to tell her what kind of exquisite material she was wearing. The woman stared at her. "Meal sacking," she said and moved on.

Elsie didn't see Father Courvaille among the spreading crowds, many of whom appeared to be bus tourists from nearby Harvey Houses, where they'd purchased discount tickets for today's "Indian Detour." She accepted the ladies' invitation to join them on their large white blankets.

"My dear, your foot appears to be healing," said Martha, offering each woman a green apple from one of her baskets.

"Yes, the doctor who's tending me changed the dressing yesterday. He saw no need to be quite so elaborate with fresh wrappings," Elsie said. In fact, Dr. Gonzalez had seemed in quite a hurry and she had not tarried with him; she had arrived early in the afternoon, without an appointment, and stayed just long enough to see that the fence was gone from around his compound.

Old Pueblo men wearing blue velvet shirts sat quietly next to barefooted women, wrapped in blue tablitas, on the dirt behind the blanket. Before the dancing began, a cadre of men approached Martha, Margretta, and Elizabeth. They offered the women white lilies. "We wish to extend you a special welcome for the work you have done on our behalf, establishing the Indian Arts Fund," said one of the men. He wore silver bracelets and a faded leather belt.

"Our pleasure," Martha said. She bowed.

Margretta waved Elsie onto her feet. "You're one of us!" she whispered.

Elizabeth gave a short speech to people huddled immediately around the church, impatiently awaiting the dance. She said Pueblo pottery was a brilliant indigenous art form unrecognized by the larger American culture. Granting the work its proper value would strengthen American identity and improve America's standing in the world at a time of continuing global crisis; this was the aim of the Indian Arts Fund. Along the way, she and her partners hoped, the growing appeal of Pueblo pottery would ensure the community's financial security.

Elsie felt foolish standing arm-in-arm with the women. This was the first she'd heard of the Indian Arts Fund. Bryn Mawr (and Old Money) strikes again! she thought. She'd done nothing to deserve any honors. She was no different than the Harvey House hordes staring uncomprehendingly around the plaza.

Behind her, a Pueblo elder muttered, "Why do these women care about us? Don't they have children at home?" A companion answered him in Tewa, and Elsie lost the conversation.

Across the church's stone terrace she glimpsed Father Courvaille. He stood in a knot of onlookers, watching her. She couldn't read his expression. He wore his white collar. On duty.

A ribbon of dancers unwound into the open then, from around the corner of an alley, chanting to a drumbeat. Fifty voices or more. On their heads, a jittering storm cloud of brown eagle feathers. The men waved fox furs and branches. In double file they came, old and young, nude (skinny and fat, bulbous and long), ocher, painted with clay. They were followed by blue-striped men. Bandoliers made of scalloped white shells draped their chests. Pine limbs spiked their arms, parrot feathers gilding their long black hair. Their moccasins kicked up yellow caliche. The drums thudded as dully as automobile tires thumping wet asphalt. With rattling gourds, the dancers mimed the sounds of quick thunderstorms.

Next, women in tablitas entered the crowded plaza. Watching their elaborate head gear shimmy was like witnessing the stones of a Spanish cathedral fly apart, reassemble, then fly apart again. With their bare feet they beat forth grains and seeds from the earth. They circled a hand-held scale model of an arbor attached to a board. It had been designed using evergreen cones, cornstalks, and cottonwood. Beneath the arbor's shade, a tiny plaster Catholic saint, palms bleeding, consulted a wooden sundial.

Lovely Mexican boys singing dance tunes that will lift you, spinning, into the air. Willa's voice pulsed in Elsie's mind along with the drums' hypnotic rhythms. As far as Elsie knew, Willa had never attended a Corn Dance; *she* was captivated by the Mexican fiestas. Elsie couldn't imagine Willa waltzing to the strumming of guitars, but she'd sworn that one evening a gorgeous singer had coaxed her onto her feet at a fire-lit *afuera*. She said she'd wished, that night, dawn would never break above the mesas.

Now, through the legs of bobbing dancers, Elsie watched a woman on the terrace. In dappled sunlight the woman was busy arranging a row of micaceous red pots. Presumably, she would sell the pottery to tourists, along with cups of atole, once the dancing was over. The pots glowed, the way Willa's pieces had shone on the mantel of her Bank Street apartment.

A lithe Eagle Dancer stepped into the plaza. Muscles rippled the billows of his shirt. Curved, feathered poles gave him magnificent wings. He went careening through the crowds like a carving come to life, gliding from the side of a cliff.

Suddenly, four women wearing blue skirts whirled to the edge of the blanket where Elsie lay. The dancers mimed the picking of crops, hunching and stooping to the drumbeats. Four *kachinas*, gaudy clowns, faces painted red, pounced upon the women, lifted their skirts, and stuck their heads between their legs—right in front of Margretta! Then the crop women straddled the clowns. Elizabeth whispered to Martha, "Are they doing what I *think* they're doing?"

"They appear to be . . . my god, they're suggesting the act of cohabitation!" Martha exclaimed. "Why—oh my dear!—it's as lurid as jazz dancing!"

Genuinely shaken by that final performance, Margretta, Martha, and Elizabeth left the plaza quickly, gathering lilies, blankets, umbrellas, and baskets. On the way out, Elizabeth urged Elsie to attend an upcoming meeting of the Indian Arts Fund. They'd be discussing promotional strategies for Pueblo crafts, she said, as well as their response to rumors that legislators, here and in Washington, were illegally blocking Indian land claims. "We'll be in touch."

When the ladies had departed, Father Courvaille limped over. "All that frenetic movement!" he said. "Just *watching* it stirs my gout." He bought her an atole. He stuck with his flask. For the next half hour, he introduced her to many people of the Pueblo, as well as to Mexican laborers and a few Anglo farmers who'd attended the dance with their families. Each person greeted him with considerable deference, but more striking to Elsie was the depth of the affection they reserved for him. He appeared to be a favored uncle rather than a stern religious counselor. Only once did he assume the traditional role of a priest. It happened in an instant. A weeping woman approached him rocking an obviously sick baby in her arms. The infant was jaundiced, too weak to cry. Father Courvaille knelt with the woman in the dirt, and he placed his hands on her head and around the baby's skull. He prayed silently, his lips barely moving. As he did so he seemed to grow physically in eminence and in size, a transformation as astonishing as the boy-become-an-eagle.

The woman thanked him. She disappeared behind the church. Elsie said, "It's remarkable to me . . ."

"What?"

"How you split yourself . . . your, I don't know, your personality . . . forgive me, but I mean . . ."

"The sacred and the profane." Father Courvaille laughed. "One is not possible without the other, my dear. You see, I know myself." He tipped his flask to his lips.

Through those lips have passed the Word of God, Elsie thought. "And by that I suppose you mean to say I *don't* know myself?"

"I'm suggesting it's in the nature of a reformer to be dissatisfied. Restless. Maybe even displaced—*wherever* she finds herself. Your friends," he said. "This art fund they've started? You're going to join them?"

"So far, I've had nothing to do with their politics. I just arrived, remember?"

"Preserving the hut. Changing your life entirely . . ."

"What's wrong with helping these people?" Elsie said impatiently. "*You* do it."

"I belong to this community."

"And it's okay to keep others out?"

"Just be careful, Miss Sergeant. Consider, thoroughly, what you're doing. That's all I'm saying. You know, in my profession . . . many young priests fall prey to the notion that God has endowed them to become people's saviors. To the contrary. We're servants. It's a great mistake to believe we're above those we try to lift. I would hate to see you fall into that error."

With her cane, Elsie sketched an infinity sign in the dirt. "I'm rather offended you'd think I would."

Father Courvaille nodded at two Pueblo women, walking their little girls to the church. "This scheme your friends have cooked up . . . 'recognizing' the value of Indian art while seeking to enrich the Pueblos. Do you not see a conflict of interest there?"

"I'm not—"

"Are they museum curators or businesswomen? Critics or brokers? Assigning 'value' to pieces from which they are likely to profit?"

"You're being unfair."

"Am I? And the Pueblos? Are they now elevated to the status of artists? Or do they merely provide commodities to wealthy white patrons?"

"But they're already doing it! Women were selling pots out there today!"

"Yes, and tourists were bused in to watch what is essentially a religious ceremony." He shook his head.

"You think I'll make things worse."

"I think you must take great care in finding your place here."

"I must say, Father Courvaille." Elsie laughed bitterly. "You *do* have a habit of hectoring me. Now tell me: why *is* that?"

A genial shrug. "I know from reading your magazine pieces that you're a thoughtful woman. If you'll pardon me for saying so, your friends strike me as reckless."

"Lost causes?"

"Perhaps."

He raised his flask again. Elsie tapped it. "I would have thought you didn't believe in lost causes."

"Touché," he said.

"And as for the sacred and profane . . ." She asked him about the bawdy routine, the red-faced clowns, the "naughty" dance following the somber fertility rites earlier in the day. "One cannot exist without the other?"

"Precisely."

"Like art and commerce?"

He laughed. "It's always a pleasure to speak with you, Miss Sergeant."

"And you."

"Good luck with your construction."

Ramon and Matías had been squabbling all morning. "That fellow, he no *sabe* two-by-four!" Matías yelled.

"Matías, please just replaster the dining room wall. I'll take care of the two-by-fours, okay?" Elsie said.

"Está bueno, patrona. Muy bien."

She would rather have lolled in the sunshine like a purring cat than continue working, but the men needed constant mediation. They'd fallen out of sorts after complimenting her on her mobility. In passing, she'd mentioned Dr. Gonzalez. Ramon had muttered, "He weak, after all." He spat on the ground.

"Yes, I noticed his fence was gone."

Afterward, she regretted her comment. Apparently, her biggest mistake was not choosing sides in the land war. For the rest of the day the men stared hard at her.

Around midafternoon, a portly gentleman came trotting up the hill riding a ragged sorrel. He looked like a country undertaker. His belly strained the buttons of his black topcoat.

He introduced himself as Señor Francisco Jemenez, the local mayordomo. He said his job was to apportion water use in the area.

"But . . . I thought anyone could draw on the irrigation ditches?" Elsie said.

"Oh no no no," said the sweating potentate. "Far from it, señora. Decisions must be made. The water is so essential to every farmer, you see."

"I don't need much now, of course, but I hope someday to plant a chili and alfalfa field, and—"

"I have concerns about certain constructions you are making here. In relation to the ditches."

It was not clear to Elsie how anything she planned could affect the acequia. The more the man tried to explain, repeating "quality" and "direction," the less sense he made. Soon, it became apparent he was waiting for her to offer him something—a "gift" to allay his "concerns" and make him go away. She went into the hut. She brought back a sack of small oranges. "For your children, perhaps? Do you have children?" she asked. What he really wanted was for her to buy his sorrel. "Fervently, I wish you to have him," he said. "I see you have great need for a pack animal."

She had no such need, but she sensed it would not do to refuse him—not just now. She might have to negotiate with this man in the future. "I'll consider it," she said. "But please, could you come back another day when we have less to do here? Our buckets of mud are drying, and I must get this finished before dusk."

"Of course, señora." He tipped an imaginary hat, turned, and trotted down the hill on his damned old horse.

4

She half woke, still moving through dreams, hovering like a dragon-fly over a black mountain lake surrounded by tufted lava cones—a lake in which the predawn stars reflected so sharply on the water the mildest ripples snagged on the mirrored burrs of light. It was as though night, in a final desperate gesture before fading, had strewn its finest diamonds among the currents. Tesuque crickets *chrr*ed, a vibration more felt than heard. If phosphorescence could make a sound, the noise might resemble something like this, Elsie thought.

Now she'd come fully awake. The crickets weren't in her dreams; they were real. Gauguin's naked brown women spread before her, the pages of the open book tittering in a warm morning breeze through the window. Something else: a crackle, a spurt of breath like steam escaping rock seams.

The walls! They were buckling all around her. Surely a lingering effect from the dreams. No. Again, a *cra-ack*! A bulge appeared at the top of the bedroom wall, a blister, a distended belly, sending creases, each with its own frightening tributaries, throughout the crumbling adobe. Plaster pelted the floor.

By midmorning her harshest fears had been confirmed. Ramon and Matías admitted—under pressure—they'd not done a proper job. (They blamed "bad mud.")

"So you'll replaster?" Elsie asked.

The men shuffled their bare feet, a pathetic vaudeville act. "No, *patrona*," said Ramon.

"What, then?"

"It must come down."

"This part? Here?"

"All of it," Matías said, barely audible.

"All of *what*?"

"All new walls." Bedroom, kitchen, the south side of the dining room.

A faint phrase skittered through Elsie's mind: a sentence she'd overheard spoken by a rancher one night in the hotel lobby. He'd been complaining about his Mexican field hands: "I swear, they get me so mad, sometimes I think if they had fur on, I'd shoot 'em."

She hated herself for dredging up these words.

Ramon and Matías had caused the problem, but she had no one else to fix it. She must hold her tongue. They estimated a week and a half, two weeks . . . depending on how full the ditches got and how quickly they could mix new mud. The brief rainy season had begun (usually an accursed time for adobe building, but fortunate, perhaps, in this circumstance); rumors had reached Tesuque that flooding had endangered upland valleys. Often, flash floods washed out downstream channels, leaving them dry, approximating severe drought. Elsie could not acclimate herself to the contradictions of aridity. One extreme condition led to another.

"Perhaps the mayordomo will help with the water," said Ramon.

Elsie nodded. She'd have to purchase that damned animal after all!

Matías warned her that "the *bailes*" would delay things further. He explained that he and Ramon played fiddle and banjo at community dances. Several *fiestas* had been scheduled in the coming weeks, to celebrate the "streaming heavens."

Accepting her helplessness, Elsie threw her bag in the Ford and drove to Santa Fe.

At the lobby desk she found a letter awaiting her, along with the latest issue of *The New Republic*. Willa had published an essay in the magazine, an examination of the aesthetics of novel writing. "Naturally, when I composed the piece, you were foremost in my mind," said Willa's letter. "Please consider my essay my earnest prod to you: *Write a novel!*"

Sitting on the bed in her room, feeling chastised, Elsie gripped the letter until her knuckles ached. Then she relaxed: Willa was just being Willa. The curtains were drawn against the fierce contest outside between rain showers and the low afternoon sun.

Willa wrote that she'd been hospitalized for a tonsillectomy. She'd spent several weeks recuperating in a sanatorium where the food resembled "black, organic obstructions removed from some poor wretch's colon." The sanatorium was perched on the outskirts of Wernersville, Pennsylvania. It had been recommended to Willa "as the best of the worst sorts of places to be."

Next to the sanatorium, a pharmacy occupied the ground floor of a brownstone, she said. Its back room doubled as a cobbler's studio. There, a wizened old man repaired hobnail boots and stitched silk-white baby slippers. The combined smells of the philters and powders in the front room—mustard, hyssop, salts and gums, blue crystals, bay leaves, lime flowers, corn silk—had seeped into the cobbler's leather over time, infusing shoe tongues with an odor similar to sugared lemons. Stopping by the chemist's one day to retrieve a prescription, Willa said, she had peered past the thin red curtain to the room in back. The shoemaker's shelves burst with stiff wooden feet: models taken from former patrons of the shop, most of whom were long deceased. For many years, the chemist explained, he had been lax in his cleaning and organizational habits. Willa had stood there gazing at the feet of the dead: a form of mummification. Her skin went cold. "Dearest Elsie, I thought of you then. I don't know how you survived that sick ward in Paris. The wounded and the dying . . . it seems that weakness requires more strength than I will ever be able to muster!"

As a postscript, she added, "Oh, . . . and speaking of the sick ward: my editor has finally mailed a copy of my war book, *One of Ours*, to you; it will arrive any day now fresh from the publisher's lair. I do hope it meets with your approval. You understand, better than anyone, the cruel nature of its subject. Which is why I ask again: when will you write *your* novel?"

Why did Elsie feel (not for the first time) that Willa was not praising her literary potential but rather belittling her hard-earned reporting skills?

Willa's essay, "The Novel Demūeblé," affirmed her suspicion. "If the novel is a form of imaginative art, it cannot be, at the same time, a vivid and brilliant form of journalism," Willa had written. "Out of the teeming, gleaming stream of the present it must select the eternal material of art."

The Indian Arts Fund needed little ink and paper to round out its membership roll. Elsie agreed to attend a meeting; she discovered that, besides Margretta, Martha, and Elizabeth, the group consisted of what Elizabeth called an "aspirational demographic."

"You mean, you hope to recruit," Elsie said.

"One day, *all* Americans will bond and band together," Elizabeth responded.

The ladies had gathered in a former ecclesiastical residence south of Tesuque, on a half-acre once devoted to fermenting grapes. These grapes were intended for holy wine and wine to sell to fill the church's coffers, a vexed enterprise given God's stingy apportionment of rich soil and annual rainfall in the region. Still, a stern test and very bad wine strengthened a man's soul, said the young bishop whose residence this place had been for many years. He had bottled enough product to establish his power in the diocese. He had used his position to reorganize the local church hierarchy, undoing the former bishop's vision of reaching impoverished souls in the remoteness of the desert. Instead, the younger bishop felt a calling to replicate Heaven on Earth. He would create a fresh New World Garden, terraced like a natural staircase. Here, pilgrims, having committed to an arduous journey, could revitalize the sacred seeds nestled within them. He fashioned the half-acre and the residence into a splendid, if spare, oasis. If the wine was bitter, it was nevertheless finely packaged—in glass blown by exquisite craftsmen, featuring labels as colorful as French oil paintings hanging in small museums.

The house resembled a toy palace. More carpets adorned the walls than covered the floors. Arched interior doorways projected the illusion of height. In another age, another place, visitors might have mistaken the candelabra for a collection of bear traps.

Now, many years later, long after the house had left the church's hands and become a public meeting hall, it no longer inspired the pinched awe that imitation greatness sometimes evokes. Elsie found it drab and cold, emptied of its former furnishings except for some high-backed chairs and a handful of carved pieces from an elaborate old Nativity scene. Nothing sadder than former glory, she thought. Stories of the young bishop's power ploys gave the dwelling an even glummer air, a taint of banality. Elsie supposed that, to a finer sensibility, politics was to religion as journalism was to literature. You may bottle them in similar containers, but certain vintages outshone the rest.

Following her first meeting with the Indian Arts Fund, she would spend several weeks helping the ladies plan "actions" against New Mexico's U. S. Senator Holm O. Bursum and his Washington partners. Bursum had introduced federal legislation ratifying all non-Indian claimants' stakes for land they said they'd squatted on prior to 1902.

To Elsie, these "actions" were not the politics of banality but rather a crusade for justice. There *was* a difference—though she doubted an aesthete like Willa would recognize it. In the past, whenever Elsie had tried to explain to her friend the problem of Pueblo land rights, Willa had waved her hand dismissively—"You know I don't care about such matters"—though she had always expressed reverence for the ancient dwellings at Mesa Verde. She spoke of her melancholy over the loss of such a noble and simple way of life.

Along with Paul Gauguin, Elsie decided, Willa might say, "I close my eyes in order to see."

Many months later, after the Pueblos had won their battle with Bursum, Elsie reflected that she would always think fondly of that period in her life. She associated her "actions" with the meeting hall's crudely carved Nativity scene, in whose presence she'd helped hatch many of the Arts Fund's strategies. Ever since the Catholics had abandoned the house, Pueblo children had added pieces to the sacred tableau—the blocky wooden sheep, the faceless shepherds—so now *kachinas* danced above the Christ child next to the Wise Men, beavers and elk joined camels in silent commemoration of the world's salvation.

Senator Bursum—an obviously odious man whom Elsie hoped never to meet—had neglected to tell the Pueblos he had authored the land bill and secured its initial passage in a Senate subcommittee. The Arts Fund's first strategic move was to call a meeting of the Tesuque, Taos, Isleta, Zuni, San Felipe, and Laguna governors, to warn them of the danger they faced. In anger, the men shook their power sticks. If Elsie mistook one of their staffs for her cane one night, and took it home with her, she might command the thunder and the rain, she thought, lava floods melting the Earth's surface, the sun's flaming tongues setting lights a-dance in the sky.

The governors understood that any court system overseen by white men would erase Pueblo rights, though Pueblo land stakes preceded by many years the claims of Anglo and Mexican squatters.

"King Philip the Second of Spain instituted the Laws of the Indies many hundreds of years ago," said the Tesuque governor. "Those laws promised a good future for Indians throughout the vast domain of Spain. President Abraham Lincoln extended their authority." He admitted that none of the tribal leaders had ever learned to read Spanish. He conceded that white lawyers from the East could easily take advantage of the Pueblos' ignorance in court.

Elsie sat with the men and drafted for them a statement to be sent to the United States Congress:

Now we discover that the Senate has passed a bill, called the Bursum Bill, which will complete our destruction, and the Congress and the American people have been told that we, the Indians, have asked for this legislation to settle New Mexico's land disputes. This, we say, is not true. We have never asked for this legislation. We were never given a chance of having anything to say or do about this bill. We have studied the bill over and found that this bill will deprive us of our happy life by taking away our lands and water and will destroy our Pueblo government and our customs which we have enjoyed for hundreds of years, and through which we have been able to be self-supporting and happy down to this day.

Elsie wrote letters to *The Nation* and *The New Republic* informing readers that "New Mexico entered the United States in 1846 but Pueblo lands remained in Pueblo hands. President Lincoln upheld and defended their sovereignty. The Pueblos have never been herded onto reservations the way the Plains Indians were when they lost their hunting grounds. By maintaining their alluvial fields and forest trails, the Pueblos have always been economically independent."

For its second initiative in favor of Indian rights, the Arts Fund relied on its original mission: to promote Pueblo pottery—not only as an art form but also as a symbol of self-determination. The message was simple. The pottery was part of America's great cultural heritage. And it was an economic boon to a traditionally impoverished region. Bursum's legislation would harm us all, not just an overlooked minority.

The strongest opposition to the group's activities came from Catholic schoolteachers, women who had long taught in the Southwest's "Indian" schools. The teachers agreed—the Pueblos had a right to prosper. But their future was best ensured through the process of assimilation into European/Christian culture. Indigenous languages, Native arts, and insular social practices were terribly counterproductive, the teachers said; the only sensible way forward for the Indians was through full American citizenship.

The Bryn Mawr ladies mulled this point for several nights in the candlelit darkness of the ecclesiastical house. Elsie felt that *some* form of American citizenship should be considered if it didn't cost the Pueblos their heritage or their land.

For *The Nation* she wrote, "One U. S. Indian Agent I spoke to told me that, in matters of land disputes between the Pueblos and the state of New Mexico, the Indians are 'children.' But the Indians at Tesuque, with their corn-grinding stones, their three-cornered open cooking fires, and their river-water jars carried delicately atop their heads, are, rather, the Children of the Ages."

5

In the midst of Elsie's "actions," Dr. Jung arrived in Santa Fe. She had first met Dr. Jung in Zurich, in 1904, shortly after he had established his medical practice at the Burghölzli Psychiatric Clinic. She had approached him both as a patient and as a writer, curious about the impact of his work on her psyche *and* her career. The latter got a boost when she published an article on the clinic in *Harper's*. Her psyche remained, to her, a seething swamp.

One day he told her she was "like an egg without a shell," experiencing the world primarily through feelings and intuitions rather than sense impressions or thinking. If this was meant to help her, it did not.

She *did* feel safe in his sober, book-lined study, lighted by afternoon sunshine through a stained-glass window, the walls prim with spare Oriental paintings. She liked ringing the brass bell outside his room, announcing her arrival; she liked telling him her dreams as he smoked a meditative pipe and stroked the hair of his black poodle, who made a quiet, shaggy appearance at every session. "You look more like a stockbroker than a prophet," she said one day but got no rise from the doctor. On another occasion, she challenged him, "People must lie to you all the time."

"Yes," he agreed calmly, "all men are liars, certainly. I just let them sit in that chair and lie till they get tired of lying. Then they begin to tell the truth."

He seemed to appreciate her boldness, her refusal to accept appearances (*intuiting*, perhaps, something deeper). One afternoon he began to confide in her, providing the basis for her article. "In the world of my childhood, on the shore of Lake Constance in

Switzerland, it had been taken for granted that there was nothing preposterous or world-shaking in the idea that there might be events which overstepped the limited categories of space, time, and causality," he said. "Animals were known to sense beforehand storms and earthquakes. There were dreams which foresaw the deaths of certain persons, clocks which stopped at the moment of death, glasses which shattered at the critical moment. But as a young man, seeking my education in the great cities of Europe, I was apparently the only person who had ever heard of these phenomena. In all earnestness I asked myself what kind of world I had stumbled into. It seemed to me a place of denial. Plainly, the urban world knew nothing about the country, the real world of mountains, woods, rivers, of animals and 'God's thoughts' (plants and crystals). It became clear to me that humanity's problems stemmed from the fact that most of us were ruled by our unconscious."

For the rest of her stay in Zurich, Elsie asked the doctor far more questions than he asked her. He relaxed in her presence. She would arrive at his house, a square stone building looking like a medieval stronghold, and catch him washing his clothes in a tub of soapy water. They would talk together for hours. They became friends. When she landed in New Mexico, one of the first things she did was telegraph him about the Pueblo cosmos. She knew the details would intrigue him.

When she met him at the station, stepping off the Atchison, Topeka, and Santa Fe, she was relieved to see his brown eyes remained keen after all these years, his arms powerful, swinging his bags, his face ruddy and bright.

Standing by the train in a little cloud of steam, he gave a cry of distress at the sight of her cane. "Tell me, my dear, are you refighting the war here in the Wild, Wild West?" he said.

She settled him into his room at the hotel. They spent the rest of that day at a table in the restaurant discussing, over tea and biscuits, the Pueblo concept of the belly as the seat of thought. Forget the heart, the mind. At one point, Dr. Jung interrupted the conversation to exclaim that "certainly, civilized man" remained "archaic at the deepest levels of his psyche."

The anxiety Elsie had felt prior to his visit—fear that his European manners would stir painful memories of France for her, that he would not be as fascinated as she had hoped he would be with Native beliefs—evaporated along with the steam from the tea.

Toward evening, as blue shadows rolled across the plaza, tinting the hotel windows, Elsie looked up and saw Mountain Lake standing stiffly next to their table. He wore a buckskin jacket. Its white lines deepened the copper hue of his skin. A faint sage smell rose from the folds of his clothes.

"How did you know?" Elsie began.

"I told you I would come." She thought again: *If he's playing a part, he does it with great panache.*

"Dr. Jung, Ochwiay Bianco."

The doctor rose and bowed.

For the next three hours, Elsie sat quietly as the Pueblo chief explained his universe to the European doctor. She wondered what each man thought of the other. "The sun is God—everyone can see that," Bianco said. "We help our father go across the sky. We do this not only for ourselves, but for the world. If we were to cease our practices, in ten years' time the sun would no longer rise. Then it would be night forever."

Dr. Jung clapped his hands, delighted. Mountain Lake crossed his arms on his chest. "How can there be another god?" he said. "Nothing can be without the sun. What would a man do alone in the mountains? He cannot even build his fire without him."

"So when you come into town," said Dr. Jung. "When you witness—"

"The Americans want to stamp out our religion. Why can they not let us alone? What we do, we do for the Americans also. Everyone benefits by it. If we did not do it, what would become of the world?"

"From your point of view, then, white men—"

"White men are always seeking something. What are they seeking? They are uneasy and restless. We do not know what they want. We do not understand them. We think they are mad."

The men talked late into the night, each fulfilling his archetypal—his *clichéd*?—role, Elsie thought: the Wise Elder, the Refined Cosmopolitan. The other restaurant guests paid their bills and left. Finally, after a brief lull in the conversation, Mountain Lake rose without ceremony, nodded solemnly to Elsie, and walked to the door.

Dr. Jung ordered two brandies. The weary staff wanted to shut the place, but he needed to ponder. "To be sure, he was caught up in his world just as much as a European is trapped in his, but what a world!" he said. "This experience, Elsie—it was not like glimpsing an alien shore. No. It was like discovering new approaches to age-old knowledge, almost forgotten."

He mused, "Roman legions smashing the cities of Gaul, St. Augustine thrusting Christianity upon the Britons with the tip of a spear, Charlemagne's forced conversions of the 'heathen,' Columbus, Cortes . . . what *we* have called civilizing crusades, Mountain Lake's people called assaults. Merciless attacks performed by birds of prey. Who is to say this simpler explanation is not the more truthful one?

"'Who is to say the sun is *not* God? Everyone can see that,'" Dr. Jung repeated. "Indeed." He swallowed the last of his drink.

The following day—his final and only full day in New Mexico—he spent on the plaza square consolidating notes on his conversation with Mountain Lake; in years to come, these notes would form the basis of an article he would title "The Spiritual Problem of Modern Man."

Elsie marveled at how quickly he could arrive at a grand vision and be so certain of himself. He was like Willa that way. Elsie hoped she had done the right thing, introducing the men. While the doctor wrote his notes, she was content to sit on a nearby bench composing new pieces, for *The Nation* and *The New Republic*, attacking the Bursum Bill.

She would never see Mountain Lake again.

The next morning she walked Dr. Jung to his train. He was going to California. He thanked her for bringing him to the great Southwest. "It was a most enlightening experience," he said. "You know, I was thinking last night, after our day's long talk. It's through the symbols and music of art that those of us who consider ourselves 'civilized'—but who are really just crusted over with long habit—most easily access the 'primitive,' the essential ties to the world our friend Bianco expressed so eloquently." He raised Elsie's hand to kiss it. "You, my dear, are an artist. Treasure your gift of words."

She promised him she would. The most remarkable thing about Dr. Jung? Physically, he never looked the same way twice. In an instant, his facial contours could shift into an expression you'd not seen before. You'd wonder if you'd actually ever met the man. "'Out of life comes death and out of death life,' Heraclitus wrote," said Dr. Jung. "Bianco reminded me of his words—their views have much in common. Out of the young comes the old, and out of the old the young." He tipped his hat. He stepped onto the train. "The stream of creation and dissolution? Elsie, my dear, it never stops!"

6

In early summer, Elsie's magazine pieces spurred the United States Congress to send an invitation to the Pueblo governors. The Senate Committee on Public Lands and Surveys asked the tribal leaders to testify about the Bursum Bill. Secretary of the Interior Albert Fall personally extended his welcome to the "Natives."

Margretta insisted that Elsie accompany the men back east, not only because she had raised their national profiles, but also because she knew this part of America—the "arrogant part of the country" that commanded (or *thought* it did) the rest of the continent.

Following the Washington trip, the governors were invited to attend the opening morning ceremonies of the New York Stock Exchange—an opportunity arranged by New York media for the benefit of New York journalists, desperate for an exotic angle in this otherwise arcane story about a faraway desert.

Willa remained in Pennsylvania, at the sanatorium recovering from her tonsillectomy, so Elsie would not see her. Perhaps just as well, given Elsie's activities. Doubtless, Willa would not have approved of them. ("When are you going to write a *novel*?") The trains would take just short of a week to cover the broad expanse of America—the flat Texas plains, the red hills of Oklahoma, where light conveyed the crushing intensity of space.

Congress turned out to be an entirely forgettable experience: a series of soul-killing meetings with spoiled, dyspeptic men. Conversely, the Stock Exchange proved unexpectedly memorable.

A rule forbade speeches on the floor. The Pueblos sang and played their drums instead, beneath white numbers on the black Exchange board, clattering across thin wire rollers. The numbers resembled strange runic symbols deep inside a cave dwelling.

Women weren't allowed on the floor but Elsie, wearing a long, shapeless coat, managed to sneak past the guards—amid the blinding pop of flashbulbs—during the governors' entrance. Men stood scratching their bald spots in a swirl of discarded paper on the floor. Elsie overheard one broker say to another, "My god, we've got an Indian uprising right here in lower Manhattan!"

These men were familiar New York types to her. She used to lunch near Wall Street after leaving Willa's Village apartment. Watching the brokers, she asked herself frankly if she missed the city's electric atmosphere. Somewhat surprisingly, the answer was no. She had made a new life among the mesas, among the adobe walls painted with shadows and light. She had become a Westerner.

7

Willa's war novel arrived at the Wasiolek Manor Hotel on a Tuesday afternoon in early August. The cottonwoods were aflame. Ramon and Matías had just left town. They had come to tell Elsie that the walls were nearly finished and to remind her that she owed the mayordomo for his horse. She had agreed to purchase the nag in exchange for extra water. She wondered what the Stock Exchange would make of the West's casual bartering habits.

She told Ramon and Matías she would drive out tomorrow to inspect their work. She had just bought a salmon-colored Spanish chest at an antique store on the plaza (another bill to pay!). She thought it would find its rightful spot between the hut's dining room door and the fireplace, next to her bookcase. She was eager to begin the interior decorating. Meanwhile, the plaza was abuzz with Pueblos from Taos and Tesuque buying provisions for the next Corn Dance—a celebration of summer, the dance of full fruition, in contrast to the spring parade in honor of germination. This time, the performers would not invoke a soft spring patter but rather a volcanic flood—the force of fat yellow ears of corn exploding their lush green sheaths. She was sorry Dr. Jung could not return to see the dancers.

She sat on an outdoor bench, watching Pueblo women wander to and fro in their moccasins and ocher buckskins. She opened the package from Alfred A. Knopf, Willa's new publisher. *One of Ours*, said the book cover: "More and more we have come to recognize in Willa Cather our greatest living woman novelist. Here, you will say, is an authentic masterpiece—a novel to rank with the finest of this or any age."

It took Elsie only a few minutes, reading randomly, to feel otherwise. Sentimentality seemed to bleed from the binding, as if Willa had taken her tone from U.S. Treasury posters. Prevalent during wartime, the posters had been designed to inspire patriotism: "Women of America, Save Your Country, Buy War Savings Stamps!" Beneath the words, Joan of Arc, boasting an armored breastplate, lifted a sword in salute.

Willa's novel portrayed American GIs as modern equivalents of sainted Joan, salvaging Europe from barbarian hordes. The boys carried their pure pioneer spirit straight from the Great Plains into the teeth of the enemies' mechanized killing equipment. Willa's hero, a soldier based on her cousin, died—unconvincingly—with a bullet through the heart while trying to save his men. In sacrifice he found his purpose in life.

"Behind the personal drama in the novel there is an ever-deepening sense of national drama, of national character, working itself out through individuals and their destiny," the publisher had written on the dust jacket: the sort of naive hyperbole Willa would have laughed at, once, as a hardened editor warning Elsie to strive for accuracy in her writing.

The novel seemed deeply out of key, its hopeful vision of battles a mockery of the maimed and the dead, of Elsie's own wounds from the Marne. Willa had taken the world's greatest tragedy and exploited it for the purposes of her art—for her own self-importance. Her refusal to heed Elsie's warnings, the warnings of others, about the *realities* of warfare felt arrogant. Cold-hearted. Willa moved in her own inflexible direction, powerful, sometimes alarming, oblivious to what others found significant. Was this really what it took to be an artist? "Life was so short that it meant nothing at all unless it was constantly reinforced by something that endured; unless the shadows of individual existence came and went against a background that held together," Elsie read in the book. She slipped the novel back into its brown paper wrapping and sealed up the package.

The white living room walls, lighted by candles in tin sconces, reminded Elsie of the walls she had seen years ago in European dance halls. Sicily, carnival season: in the halls, peasant women and children pressed their bodies against each other shyly, seeking warmth.

The work pleased her—Ramon and Matías had earned her respect at last. The damask tablecloth she had bought some time back, along with the rose-and-white Mexican blanket she had picked up in Santo Domingo, complemented the dining room's dull pink window frames while deepening the browns of the ceiling beams and the oval table. The big Mexican cabinet standing in the corner, rather like a French armoire, now beige in color, would look much better painted green, she thought. The darker hue would highlight the perforated flower patterns in its flat tin panels. The only serpents in her garden took the shape of bees, nesting in the *vigas* outside. Ramon had gone to town for *medicina* to eradicate them.

Even the mayordomo's sorry old horse pleased Elsie on this sunny August morning. Her foot felt much better; she would strengthen it by stretching it in a stirrup.

She stood considering strategies for moving the cabinet to the center of the room, so she could paint it, when Father Courvaille appeared in her doorway, a dust cloud of whiskey fumes. His right hand appeared to hold a multipage document bound in twine. He cleared his throat. "It's been a while," he said. "I hope you don't mind. I saw your car from down the hill."

"You keep dropping by, hoping to see me roll into a ravine, is that it?"

He laughed. "Actually, I was on my way to your friend Margretta's house when I noticed your Ford." He waved the papers in his hand. "Your little group needs to be aware of this report. How *is* your foot, by the way? You seem much improved."

"Yes. Dr. Gonzalez will remove the last of the bandages on Friday. Tea?"

"Please."

"What is this report?"

He raised the title page: *An Examination of Indian Autonomy and Its Relationship to Immorality in Pueblo Dances.* "We all received copies of it—community leaders in business, in government, in the churches," he said. "It was even sent to the Bureau of Indian Affairs. Their Commissioner, a Mr. Burke, I think his name is, has apparently promised to investigate its charges."

"Which are?"

"That Pueblo rituals promote immoral relations between the sexes, as well as—how do they put it?" He flipped several pages. "'Superstitions that hinder efficient agricultural production.'"

"I see. Sounds like a political document—more about land disputes than dancing."

"It could be read that way."

"And who is behind this report?"

"A union of Catholic schoolteachers."

"Ah."

Elsie lit a small fire in the corner of her still-unfinished kitchen. She placed a pot of water on a grille above the flames. While she readied the cups and saucers, Father Courvaille scanned the breasts of island women in the Gauguin book lying open on the table.

"So. These community leaders you mentioned, are they taking this nonsense seriously?" Elsie asked.

"I'm afraid so. There's been talk of banning the Corn Dance."

"No!"

He nodded. "Forbidding anyone in the Tesuque Pueblo under the age of fifty from participating in religious rites. Passing emergency laws encouraging the Indians to adopt white concepts of thrift and harvesting—all for the sake of family welfare, of course."

"Surely you don't support these proposals?"

"It doesn't matter. Witch hunts won't work—I know that. They'll only sow discord among the people I serve. This report, it's . . . it's a case of outsiders stepping into matters that don't concern them."

"So why bring it to *our* attention?" Elsie filled the cups.

The priest pulled the flask from his pocket. "Because you come under direct attack here," he said. "Among the factors cited as contributing to local immorality are the Indian Arts Fund's 'feminist ideas.'"

"Feminist!"

"Did you recently write in *The Nation* that 'female sexuality is now in flux in American society, and opportunities exist for new hopes, new visions regarding improved roles for women?'"

Elsie rubbed her eyes.

"'Wherever possible, in the workplace and in the bedroom, sexual liberation should be encouraged?'"

"Yes, but that's a completely separate issue from Indian autonomy!"

"You know that and I know that, but many people won't. The report links jazz dancing and agitating for the women's vote with 'licentiousness on Pueblo lands.'"

Elsie laughed. "No one was more shocked by that 'naughty' dance than my friends. You saw that."

The priest shrugged.

"Whatever suspicions you or anyone else has about their intimate practices, they are proper ladies," Elsie said.

"Nevertheless." Father Courvaille waved his hand.

"Well." Elsie drained her cup. "I've learned the hard way that rotten structures collapse of their internal weaknesses. That's what will happen to this report."

"Something else you should know."

"Yes?"

"The dancers at the Pueblo . . . under pressure . . . some of them said the 'bad' parts of the Corn Dance are parodies of white women's ways. 'Our dances have always been pure,' they say. 'We do not hug and touch while dancing, the way the whites do.'"

Elsie brewed more tea. "So we . . . let me be sure about this. My friends and I . . . we're being blamed for spreading 'sin' among the people we're *working* for? And in turn, the people we're trying to help accuse us of corruption? Is that it?"

"As I say. I believed you needed to be aware."

"But that ... it's so contradictory ... it's impossible ... it's ..."

"I know. Perhaps ... perhaps you can try to see this moment as the beginning of understanding."

"*Understanding*?" Elsie laughed bitterly. "My god. Of what?"

The padre reached for his flask. "Of what it means to live in a community."

Willa sent Elsie a note informing her that advance sales of *One of Ours* had exceeded the publisher's expectations, in spite of "evil" notices by H. L. Mencken and others declaring the novel ruinous with "nonsense" at the "level of the *Ladies' Home Journal*." (Cather's war was "fought, not in France, but on a Hollywood movie lot," Mencken wrote.)

This was the first time Willa had ever seriously mentioned book sales, the first time she had claimed to value sales above critical reception or her own sense of achievement. Elsie read the short note twice. She wondered if she could still be Willa's friend.

To celebrate the freeing of her foot, Elsie talked the hotel kitchen staff into letting her bake a cherry pie to take to Dr. Gonzalez. She wrapped the still-warm pie, in its glass dish, in newspaper to keep it firm and safe on her car seat. The paper's lead article addressed the "Indian problem." The writer insisted walls were necessary, boundary lines integral, to any concept of the Land of Freedom: "Without boundaries, how do we know we even *have* a country?"

She drove to Dr. Gonzalez's adobe. By all appearances, he had begun to build a new fence to replace the missing one. Ramon and Matías had given Elsie the impression he'd agreed to remove the barrier—they'd called him "weak." Had he changed his mind? Was he heartened by rumors of the report Father Courvaille had left with her?

As she pulled her car close to his lot, she saw that sections of the new fence had already been dismantled: wires cut, oak poles split in two. Chickens ran across a burned patch in the yard. Cottonwood fuzz blew across the grass. Elsie parked. One of the house's windows had been smashed.

She clutched her cane. She left the pie in the car. The front door stood ajar. Soft weeping inside, somewhere in the dark. She entered the bare room where, months before, the doctor had laid her on the wooden table. There she found the doll woman bent over the doctor's sprawled figure on the floor. He bled from a gash in his head, crimson and white, his black hair matted in a tangle of viscera. For an instant, Elsie was back in the Marne. She couldn't kneel without hurting her foot. She determined he was still breathing. "Stay here," she told the woman. "I'll bring help."

She drove to the church in Tesuque. The associate priest told her Father Courvaille was not present. Finally, aides located him on the Pueblo, administering last rites to a dying elderly man. With the priest's help, authorities transported Dr. Gonzalez to a medical clinic in town, where he lay unconscious for the next three days.

Father Courvaille kept Elsie apprised of his progress. The priest dropped by her hut in the afternoons for whiskey-spiked tea and pieces of cherry pie. He said the doctor's companion had told sheriff's deputies that two Pueblo men had tried to burn the new fence. When the doctor attempted to stop them, they struck him with the butts of their rifles, following him into the house and beating him senseless. Why he had started to erect a new fence and if he would fully recover—these were questions no one seemed able to answer.

Eventually, Elsie herself tore the wrappings off her foot, re-exposing her wounds to the world. This seemed to be her only way forward (as opposed to Willa, she thought, who'd never admit to being injured in the first place).

"Frost, he make dead the apples," said Matías, handing her a blasted black gnarl, the remains of her fledgling orchard following an unexpected early freeze around the first of October. In the lower valleys, the yellow rabbit brush, the piñon trees patching rocky slopes, sticky with cones just days ago, had shriveled in sparkling sheaths of ice. Burros, foraging for nuts—delicacies rich, sweet, and round—stumbled across rime-locked terraces. Ramon and Matías wrapped themselves in sheepskins. They built fires on the hill, their faces faun-red in the flickering light. They assured the *patrona* this early chill would not last. Its damages would be limited. She must relax and enjoy her first full autumn here.

Indeed, spiritually, the season was mostly satisfying. Elsie's pieces in the national press, publicizing the Pueblos' plight, had contributed to a shift in public favor for Native land rights. U.S. senators no longer perceived political advantage in passing the Bursum Bill. They let it die on the chamber floor. Albert Fall resigned as the secretary of the interior. The local schoolteachers—the Morality Parade, Martha called them—lost steam following the bill's defeat. Under pressure from Pueblo governors, newspaper editorialists denounced the Indian autonomy report as prejudiced and harsh. The Corn Dance had proceeded as scheduled, though Elsie, occupied with her hut, did not attend.

As she sipped tea in the gold-brown shadows of her dining room window, overlooking misted cedar woods in the valley, she considered her biggest problem: the morning frost's effects on her leg. The nerves in her wounded spots reacted sharply to any temperature drop. Her muscles had become painful barometers of atmospheric changes. Many fires this winter. Blankets and many pots of tea. She'd write letters to her friends back east, all of whom had informed her of Willa's success in spite of the drubbing her book had taken from critics. It seemed the novel's sentimentality had appealed to the families of men killed in Europe. The families did not want to believe they'd suffered ingloriously. The book had been nominated for major literary prizes, the country's attempt to feel righteous, Elsie thought. She still could not finish *One of Ours*. She had not been in touch with Willa.

Then one day a letter arrived from her editor at *Harper's*. He offered her a contract for a three-part series on salvaging and remodeling her mud hut, her "joyous discovery of the pure, primitive pleasures of the Natives' way of life."

"No!" she cried aloud, upset by the editor's language. She had not pitched her story to him couched in such treacly terms, had she? If she were to match his expectations, she'd be sentimentalizing the Pueblos as much as Willa had softened the catastrophe of Europe.

Of course, from the first, Father Courvaille had insisted her presence here was sentimental. Misguided. Exploitive. She did not belong on this hill. She did not know what she was doing, involving herself in local politics.

Perhaps he was right, she thought. Perhaps Willa's approach was the better one, after all: ignoring the specific complexities of one's time and place—instead, simplifying, shrinking the truth to platitudes. Wars *were* fought for Honor and Glory. Death in battle *was* heroic (never mind the pathetic, gruesome, nearly comic image of a severed arm flying through the air as a result of someone's stupidity).

Complexities silenced folks. In turn, simple explanations allowed them to grasp a subject well enough to talk about it. Perhaps this was the major difference between journalism and art, Elsie thought. Willa understood art's childishness. The power, the wonder of the fairy tales we awakened our minds with as kids. As an editor, she *did* always preach "paring things back." "Throw out all this silly bric-a-brac," she'd instruct Elsie, poring over her manuscript pages late in the evenings in the magazine's chilly offices. (And in fact, wasn't it Elsie's descriptions of Pueblo pottery, its beauty, its value in the marketplace—not discussions of boring legislation—that had swayed some of her recent readers to support Indian land rights?) Greatness returning to simplicity: the paradox at the heart of evolution that might signal the world's salvation.

Book Two

New York, 1940

I

Elsie had fundamentally misunderstood the problem. From her small cottage at Sneden's Landing, she had mailed Willa a walking cane, a carved oak shaft topped by a silver handle. The handle was molded into the shape of a bald eagle tightly folding its wings. An accompanying note, signed "Your loving friend," said Elsie was sorry to hear about Willa's accident. She hoped she would soon regain her "sea legs"—in any case, Elsie was surprised to learn that Willa had attended a dance. This didn't sound like Willa. Elsie teased her, "I trust this news means you're not letting the old age you often complain about slow you down."

She ended her note with a tedious description of an alcoholic priest she'd met in Tesuque two decades ago. He'd given Elsie this cane when she'd first arrived there and aggravated her old war wound. She was happy to pass the instrument on to Willa now with best wishes for a swift recovery. (Recently, Elsie said, she'd heard the old fellow had died . . . gotten drunk one night and slipped into a steep ravine . . . he'd been so kind to her.)

Dear Elsie—still in need of severe editing after all these years! She *knew* Willa wouldn't want to hear the story of a dirty old stick.

And what fool had informed her of Willa's mishap? Whoever it was couldn't separate one limb from another. (What was the vulgar expression—telling one's ass from a hole in the ground?) The trouble was Willa's right wrist. For some time now it had ached intolerably whenever she wrote. She scrawled her rough drafts, always, by hand, using a fountain pen her sweet mother had passed on to her the last time Willa saw her. Then that bleating cad, McWhinney, jerked her across the boat's wet deck at what Elsie had mistakenly called a "dance."

Later that night, in the emergency room of the French Hospital, a doctor diagnosed "serious inflammation of the sheath of the tendon." He devised a steel and leather brace for the lower half of her arm, immobilizing Willa's thumb. The rest of her fingers remained free so she could grip her pen, but writing was difficult.

Now Elsie had sent her a useless old cane!

Willa set the cane in a darkened corner of her apartment, next to the chrome-green Mexican cabinet Elsie had given her years ago when she'd relinquished her hut in Tesuque and moved all her belongings back east. The cabinet did not match the rest of Willa's turn-of-the-century furnishings, but she had always admired the piece; she suspected Elsie had passed it on to her less from generosity than necessity. Too broke to find a place in Manhattan (still freelancing, poor girl), she had been forced to rent a friend's cramped cottage far up the Hudson. She no longer had room for the larger objects she had kept in New Mexico.

The darkness in that quarter of the apartment (the windows faced the brick wall of the Colony Club next door) softened the cabinet with shadows, easing it into a proper fit with the rest of the space. When Willa and Edith first moved here eight years ago, after long transience in the city—this city that did nothing but *tear down, tear down, tear down* its cherished old structures!—Willa hated the lack of light. But now the apartment's claustrophobic atmosphere suited her. Street sounds were muffled. The place turned its back on the fashionable new boutiques appearing on both sides of Park Avenue. In this sense, Willa thought, it was an expression of her inner being. Unpacked boxes still crammed a narrow hallway just off the kitchen; after all this time, a shred of Willa's soul remained homeless, in exile, buffeted, she imagined, by a harsh prairie wind or a dust storm racing across the purple mesas of a vast Southwest desert.

Wherever she was, she would always feel a touch of home as long as she had the George Sand engraving framed on her wall and the lock of Keats's hair under glass, treasures bequeathed to her by Annie Fields, in Mrs. Fields's final days on Charles Street. Willa now thought of those days as literature's last flowering on the planet, the rooms there a rare greenhouse for ideas, a poetic herbarium, before the pestilence of modernity set in, starting with the rubble of Europe in wartime.

She picked up her pen, dropped it—her fingers trembled—and retrieved it from the floor. She began a thank you letter to Elsie. She decided not to correct her friend's misimpressions of what had happened at the boat "dance" (too much trouble) or to reveal her general dispiritedness. "Novelists, opera singers, even doctors have in common the unique and marvelous experience of entering into the very skin of another human being. What can compare with that?" she wrote, falsely cheery.

Her muscles seized up, a painful enjambment, as if someone had twisted off her hand and shoved a broken pole inside her arm. She whimpered a little in the silent apartment, squeezing back tears. If it was this hard to compose a short letter, how would she ever again write a novel?

2

She had agreed to attend the gala on the boat because her wrist ached. She was angry with herself. When Edith was here, she warned Willa to rest her hand, to take a break from writing for a day or two. A day without writing felt stillborn to Willa, as if the sun had dispersed in the midst of its rising.

Still, in deference to Edith's concern, she slowed her pace, ceased pushing herself quite so hard, and the pain *did* ease a little.

But Edith had been gone for two weeks and wasn't scheduled to return for another three. Her copywriting job at J. Walter Thompson had become onerous of late. Many overtime hours. Willa had been a thoughtless companion—in her bad moods, brought on by the wrist pain and fears that her latest ideas were too rarified to be of interest to publishers (a consequence, Willa readily conceded, of her recoil from the noisy postwar world), she had stopped picking up after herself in the apartment, stopped cooking. She had stopped talking to Edith except to complain of the new crop of "women novelists" promoted by newspaper critics or to carp about Elsie's latest reformist nonsense in *The Nation*. "Enough about the glories of the WPA!" Willa told Edith one evening over cocktails, standing before the George Sand engraving. "You'd think that by now she and those other Bryn Mawr hens would have learned the limits of social engineering. Are the Indians of New Mexico *really* any better off now than they were twenty years ago? I think not! If Elsie really wants to reform something, she should begin with her own habits. She should write something decent—abandon that terrible women's-club phraseology! Pull herself out of this *I'm-barely-scraping-by* rut she's wallowed in for years. For decades, I've been after her to begin a novel. God knows, she may not have the skills to pull one off, but she won't even try! And oh, if she tells me one more time I *must* see the latest Eugene O'Neill . . . well, if *that's* her idea of writing, all that booze and frippery and melodrama . . . no wonder she's stuck. Noise! Just more noise!"

Edith merely smiled, strained, patient, and refilled their glasses.

A week or so later she came and sat on the bed next to Willa. Willa had propped herself with pillows against the headboard and was holding a bag of ice on her wrist. She noticed how tired Edith looked, her slender eyes nearly shut with fatigue, her wiry hair unkempt. She wore no makeup. Her lips were dry. Raw. Her square jaw, usually strong and distinct, seemed to sag into the loose yellow flesh on her neck. She smelled of the city: sooty, moist. "How is it?" she asked Willa, gently touching the back of her hand where water had leaked from the bag.

"It hurts," Willa said. "How are you?" She realized she hadn't asked Edith this in quite some time.

"My dear, *you* may not need a break in this dark and dreary season, but I do," Edith said quietly. "I've been pushing too hard at work, and here at home I feel I'm just in your way these days."

"No," Willa said.

"Listen. For nearly forty years now—*forty*, right, can you believe it?—I've been your roommate, your partner, your editor, your friend." She leaned forward and kissed Willa's forehead in that soft spot just above her nose. "And I damn well intend to be your roommate, partner, editor, and friend for forty *more*. But right now I need time to myself. I'd like your permission and your blessing." She'd accrued some vacation days, she said. She'd like to travel through Europe alone, to clear her head, to renew her energy. "And I'm thinking some peace and quiet would help you get on track on a new project. What do you think?"

They talked some more over the next few days. Finally, Willa reluctantly agreed to the plan. "I'll write to you every day I'm away," Edith promised.

On a foggy Saturday morning, she departed for Port Authority wearing her red beret and a brand-new leather jacket.

In the weeks since, Willa had outlined several essays, pieces on writing and literature, on the origins of her novels, on her meetings with other writers. While waiting for the next novel to gestate, maybe she could pass the time usefully on a collection of literary considerations—like the piece she'd written years ago with Elsie in mind, "The Novel Demūeblé." The problem was, she could not get past the outline. All she'd succeeded in doing was heightening the pain in her wrist, ignoring Edith's parting warning to "pamper that arm now and then!"

Willa would pace the dim living room, in front of the big Mexican cabinet, gripping her wrist, moaning quietly at the ceiling. Angry at herself for allowing the infirmity to worsen, she was even more upset at being weak. She should be stronger, physically *and* mentally. She had no more self-patience now than she'd felt when, as a young woman, she'd accidentally infected herself with a hairpin. She'd sworn then that under no circumstances would she ever again find herself in a hospital.

Her mood deteriorated one afternoon when a postcard arrived from Naples. Edith was enjoying herself. She hoped Willa was productive and well. The card pictured Mt. Vesuvius. The volcano's conical shape nudged Willa to tears. Over thirty years had passed—still, the picture of the mountain instantly brought to Willa's dulled senses the Naples hotel room she'd once shared with Isabelle. She could smell again the salt air of the bay beneath their window. The most beautiful body of water in the world. Evenings, Mt. Vesuvius, in the distance, shifted in the gloaming from violet to lilac to purple. Willa would stand at the window, hugging Isabelle's waist, staring at the land's rocky marvels. Together, they imagined tongues of flame hurtling from the mountain, fire scorching patterns in furry earth folds, like a rancher branding his Herefords.

Now, Willa could feel again the curves of Isabelle's hips in her hands. Memory! Fiercer than any cattle herder's red-hot branding iron! Certainly, Isabelle had left her imprint on Willa. Long before Willa had met Edith, before she'd moved to New York, it was Isabelle who'd made her want to pin her hair, to stick peacock feathers in her hatbands and admit she wanted to feel special. In Pittsburgh, where Willa had moved for her first job out of college, editing bad writing for a small magazine, it was Isabelle who'd shown her the ins and outs of local society, who'd introduced her to artists, who'd invited her into her house, given Willa space and peace, in an upstairs sewing room, to write her first serious stories and poems. (The house was a precursor to the Charles Street sanctuary, Willa realized now—the kind of retreat she was always hoping to discover.) Isabelle's father, the gracious but grumpy Judge McClung, often muttered how unseemly it was for his daughter to spend so much time alone with this free-thinking woman, but no matter— Willa could always entice him to drop his guard over cocktails in the evenings. She always charmed him, and she was genuinely saddened when he began to suffer headaches, fatigue, depression—so much so that he resigned his judgeship. Doctors diagnosed "severe neurasthenia, a gap between expectations and reality."

Poor man: he didn't know what a prophet he was. Now the whole world staggered with his malady. The war had shattered *everyone's* illusions. Willa couldn't even travel to Europe now—the last time she'd embarked, shortly after the armistice, the first thing she'd witnessed were the anonymous crosses staked beneath France's pale, pink skies . . .

Memory.

The judge had been Willa's first close acquaintance consigned to the grimness of a hospital room. (*Never*, she thought, visiting him one afternoon, *never, not to me, this will never happen to me.*) Then he dropped into a stony grave.

Her parents. Her brothers. And just two years ago, dear Isabelle, the victim of a swiftly spreading liver disease.

When you reach a certain age, death rains down all around you, Willa thought, massaging her wrist, staring at the mountain

(*Isabelle's* mountain) on Edith's shiny card. She drew the velvet curtains against the brick wall next door, dimming the apartment even further.

Along with Edith's card, the day's mail had brought an invitation to a city fundraiser for the arts, to be held in a launch harbored on the East River, a gala affair featuring community leaders and persons of note: assemblymen, journalists, philanthropists, editors, artists, and writers. Usually, such occasions struck Willa as deadly beyond measure, but because of her neurasthenia (yes, call it what it was), her nostalgia (she'd first met Isabelle at an artists' ball in Pittsburgh), her loneliness for Edith, and above all her pain, from which she needed a firm distraction, she decided to dress herself to the nines and dazzle those self-important ninnies.

She pulled from her closet the red fox coat she'd bought with royalties from *One of Ours*. The rest of that money she and Edith had used as down payment, some years ago, on a summer cottage at Whale Cove on Grand Manan, in the cold Atlantic surf just off the coast of Maine. The little cape-cod cozy in the woods was her refuge now that she'd lost the McClung house (torn down after the deaths of the judge and Isabelle), lost Charles Street. And Europe.

She wrapped a purple scarf around the coat's fur collar. Always, the coat brought to her cheeks a flush of satisfaction as well as resentment. It was a warm and elegant manifestation of her novel's success, and she wore it with pride. But she could not remember the book without also recalling the excoriation of (mostly male) critics. They'd accused her of feminine ignorance, of refusing to acknowledge the brutalities of war. The worst comments she could still recite word for word: "The hero loses his life and finds his soul. We happen to believe that there is such a thing as setting too high a price even upon souls. War is too high a price."

And: "She did not know the war for the big bow-wow stuff it is. She should stick to her farms."

Silly, puffed-up men! *Bow-wow*? She'd show them. She still had some bite, if she could regain the use of her wrist.

Elsie Sergeant—now, *she* had agreed with the men. She'd never forgiven Willa for *One of Ours*, one of the many unresolved tensions in their lengthy friendship. Really—sometimes Willa wondered why she'd ever put up with that reckless girl. But then she'd remember the first time she saw Elsie, in the *McClure's* offices overlooking Madison Square Park. Elsie had come meekly offering her manuscript on tenement life. She'd reminded Willa so much of the young Isabelle: delicacy matched with strength, a potent mix of shyness and determination. From that very first day, Willa sensed they'd forever be at odds over this and that, but she also knew she'd give the girl a final pass on almost anything.

Tiny waves ruffled the hull of the launch in the harbor. City lights blazed like shining confetti against a slate-gray sky shading into the watery green of a storm. As Willa let herself be led onto the red-carpeted gangplank heading onto the boat—offering the escort her strong left arm—she caught a whiff of dampness and soot, the workaday smells Edith always brought home with her in the evenings.

Oh, how she missed her steadfast companion!

Flutes of champagne floated on aluminum trays above the on-deck crowd, trembling on the stiff, raised fingers of white-gloved waiters. Silver silk curtains fluttered through the cabins' open portholes, polished wooden ovals fore and aft, smelling of the alcohol-and-lemon oil of industrial cleansers. A small chamber orchestra seated in the stern, beneath a string of paper Chinese lanterns, played Schubert. Tow barges and turtle-shaped ferries drifted on the river, along with the Coney Island boats rocking with noisy tourists.

Willa's friend Olive Fremstad, the opera singer, was too old to perform at such gatherings now. And it was rumored that Willa's old boss from the magazine, Sam McClure—the Chief—had grown frail. She wouldn't see either of them tonight. Someone asked her the dreaded question: "What are you working on these days?"

"I'm working on obscurity and oblivion," she snapped. "It's where we'll all end up, and I'd like to perfect my approach." Everyone laughed, as if she were joking.

Gray-haired men wearing tuxes leaned against the ship's iron railings, chatting quietly about politics. Portly matrons in feathered gowns—like rows of fat piñatas—flashed their diamond earrings at each other's gleaming teeth. And here came Silas McWhinney, an obsequious little man Willa knew from her days at *McClure's*, a literary agent who made a living selling prison memoirs and exposés of prostitution rings. With him was a tub in black tie, wrangling a stogie with rubbery lips. McWhinney introduced him to Willa, Mort Percy was his name, a retired engineer with a love of the arts (and a hefty financial portfolio, Willa assumed).

"Cather! Pulitzer Prize!" he announced, inches from her face, just short of prodding her in the chest with his unlighted cigar. Willa smiled. "I loved that book! May I salute you?" Embarrassingly, he raised his hand to his brow, a private's regard for a general. Just then, an Atlantic liner steamed by, its tiers lighted like cut-glass chandeliers sailing serenely into the night. On the top decks, well-dressed families laughing and waving. Below them, in steerage, grimy wage workers, men and women, ashen and silent. All the languages of Europe seemed to mix in the brisk air above the great boat's smokestacks: Polish, German, Swiss, the blunt Bohemian lilt Willa had heard so often as a child on the Nebraska plains. "Look at them," said Mort Percy. "They wrecked their own countries, so they scramble over here looking for a hand up. Some of them, real good people, I don't deny it . . . well, let's hope they've read your book, Miss Cather, so they'll know just what our boys did for them over there."

"I'm not sure . . . that wasn't, of course, the point of my novel . . ." Willa began. The night's chill froze her wrist into a block of pain.

"You got it exactly right. If it hadn't been for our soldiers, then—"

"I only meant to show that an individual may find purpose in the most unlikely circumstances. As for any larger intention . . . I'm no supporter of war, Mr. Percy. In fact, I'm quite certain that the European conflict shattered this world. Permanently."

He chuckled, pulled a book of matches from a pocket ("Delmonico's" said the cardboard cover), and lighted his stogie. "People and things, they get shifted around by wars, but it works out for most concerned." He pointed on shore, to a six-story brownstone near Midtown. "Back in my engineering days, I helped lay that building's foundation. We had some American workers, kids mostly, and they did okay on the job. But the *real* bust-ass fellows—'scuse me—they were Italians. They wouldn'ta been here if it wasn't for the mustard gas and the bombs. Good for us, and good for them too, 'cause they came here and found a new way of life, a way of puttin' food on the table for their kids—that is, if they was willin' to become *part* of us, not like, you know, Apaches on a reservation or something." He flicked ashes over the railing into the river. Brief yellow sizzles. Then smoke. "'Course, I won't pretend it works out for everyone. Down in those holes, in the mud and the rock, preparin' to raise a building . . . sometimes you feel you're part of a swarm of animals and, you know, nothin' more than the rats at your feet. And sometimes that's true. On that very project, that building right there, the ropes, the oiled ropes holding the diamond drills and the clamshells full of sand, they was nearly worn through but none of us knew that." For a moment, measured by the bucking of a wave, he studied his glowing cigar. "The developer was cuttin' corners, refusing to spring for new cables. He knew he'd be protected by the Fellow-Servant Act if something happened. One day, a rope snapped and one of them steel clamshells came crashin' down on a group of the Italians, good men, bricklayers . . . well, I suppose *they* woulda cursed the war, in retrospect."

Willa stood quietly, gazing at the city. She shouldn't have come tonight. What do you say to such a man? She'd read once that New York construction crews employed Southwest Indians at their work sites because the Indians, used to climbing narrow mesas hunting eagles, balanced so well on steel beams in the air. She was curious to know if this was true, but she'd be damned if she'd engage Mr. Percy any further.

She followed bouncing headlights threading up and down the shoreline, past the neighborhoods she had occupied and fled in nearly forty years in New York—she remembered the cramped rooms just south of Washington Square Park where she'd first lived with Edith, torn down for medical school facilities at NYU, precipitating the first of many exiles; her lovely abode on Bank Street, a five-story house where she'd spent her happiest writing years, under Edith's watchful care, sitting near the coal grate under its white mantelpiece, listening to the daughter of the German family a floor above practice, again and again, Beethoven's *Appassionata*; initially, the repetitive musical phrases irritated Willa, but eventually she'd associated them with her working hours and missed them when the daughter wasn't home. She didn't mind carrying buckets of coal up the stairs to heat the rooms, and it didn't much bother her when the pipes froze in the winters. Then the Seventh Avenue subway came along, and the city demolished the building.

After that, Willa and Edith took temporary lodgings at the Grosvenor Hotel. "Temporary" turned out to be five years, half a decade wondering which taped box in the closet held the volumes of Dickens or her Pueblo pottery. (How it would have cheered Willa to see the red-and-white water jars she never had the heart to unpack placed around the room.)

The Grosvenor's only good quality was its proximity to the Church of the Ascension on 10th Street. After writing in the mornings, Willa would slip across the snowy avenue to the sanctuary's rounded arch. She'd sit before the altar, the great fresco depicting the Annunciation and the Vision of St. John, the Saint-Gaudens bas relief, two angels raising a chalice. She'd let the sight fill her eyes, like a tide rolling in, the tiny candles perking in their red glass cups, each flame a prayer offered against the hardness of the world, illuminating, softening the spiraling stone columns.

A flame caught her eye on shore, twisting atop a building. "My god, what is *that*?" someone said behind her. The arts crowd gathered on deck. A ball of fire swelled like an immense molten globe around the highest floors of a skyscraper somewhere on the Upper East Side. "It's the Forrester Hotel," someone whispered. They all watched as flickering red streaks cascaded through and around the structure's now-exposed girders, crumbling fast, shadows falling, flying among floating cinders. The cinders flashed as though pulsing with the force of silent screams. Gasps rose from the people on the boat. *Vesuvius. Death raining down.*

Later, reporters would write that the fire started in an attic laundry room. A faulty dryer had overheated. Thirty people perished: guests from around the world, diplomats, dignitaries, governors. Many jumped from several stories up to avoid inhaling smoke. A man's hand was discovered on a window ledge, snapped off at the wrist, as though at the last moment his fingers had refused to follow the rest of his body. The building was said to have been fireproof. Eventually, lawsuits, years in developing, would reveal that the construction firm had installed shoddy substitutes for the required materials. But on the night of the disaster, watching from the boat, Willa understood what had *really* happened: the spirit of the city had released its compressed energy, the constant upward thrust, contents under pressure, packed into the tiny space of the island . . .

Sirens echoed through the darkened street mazes. Helpless from this distance, giddy with the primal joy of *being alive*, the partiers on the launch resumed their conversations. Champagne spilled. The chamber orchestra struck up a waltz. It was then that McWhinney grabbed Willa's arm. He chirped, "Let's dance!"

Her wrist exploded in white heat—like a blistered windowpane popping on the top floor of the Forrester. She fell to the wet deck. She lost consciousness. Then she became aware of a hubbub above her. Voices conferring.

Finally, a man she understood to be an assistant editor at the *New York Times* said he had a good friend working as an emergency room doctor at the French Hospital. It was over in the Chelsea neighborhood. He was certain he could get the fellow to examine Miss Cather right away. She was lifted off the boat and into the back of a Ford.

Death was mortared into the walls of all medical facilities—Willa wasn't fooled. But despite its grim purpose the French Hospital had its charms: fleur-de-lis patterns on the front awnings, nurses not nuns, Irish, Italian, and Canadian Scotch women who botched the French language as badly as Willa did—but at least the sustaining strains of French filled the hallways. Creamy French food. Afterwards, her night in the emergency room was just a veiled impression in her mind. Doctors and nurses wielding bulky machines like those a foot soldier must encounter on a smoky battlefield . . .

She remembered a chattering nurse going on about the Sisters of the Holy Cross. She remembered the bustle of medical personnel and the smell of charred flesh—victims from the Forrester had been transported here. They had been taken to every ER in the city. It was a scene out of Dante. She remembered a young doctor examining her arm, her wrist, her hand. Amid strobing bursts of pain, she heard his gushing voice as if through a tunnel of mud: "Aside from Dos Passos' *Three Soldiers*, the one book in the world I would love to have written is *My Ántonia*. It's just superb . . . I mean . . . where did the idea come from?"

My god, just get on with it, she thought. "Homesickness," she whispered. "Endless, unbearable homesickness."

She remembered—or *thought* she recalled—meeting a man who'd barely escaped the Forrester, a self-described "adventurer." He made a living photographing the Aurora Borealis in Iceland, he said. He'd come to America to document the spectacular electrical storms flashing in Southwestern deserts. He lifted his hindquarters from the gurney he occupied next to Willa. From his back pocket he pulled a flask of rum. Had she ever been to the desert, he asked her. "Homesick," she muttered.

And then she woke in a private bed. She shook herself to woozy consciousness. An evergreen wreath studded with tiny pinecones hung, above her, on the wall. Her arm was encased in a cast.

This wasn't the first time her arm had caused her trouble. One day, shortly after completing *One of Ours*, she felt nearly paralyzed, unable to lift her pen. An internist diagnosed "neuritis" and suggested she may have assumed a sympathetic wound, having just written about so many maimed men. (In that instant, she thought of Elsie Sergeant, of the puffy red scars on her legs.) "No," she told the doctor. "It's only fatigue."

Now, a pleasant nurse adjusted her IV. She tried to engage Willa, telling a story about a flight she'd taken once on a military cargo plane, on some medical assignment. "American airmen are just wonderful!" she said, her voice high and thin. "They give me faith in this country . . . though, just between you and me, I fear the Communists have seized control of our banks now."

Within another day, Willa was back in her Park Street apartment, swallowing pain pills from a large glass bottle, massaging her wrist through her cast, sorting Edith's cards: Florence, Rome, poor, tortured Barcelona . . .

On her desk, the outlines of the essays she'd been planning: short pieces on the value of narrative restraint in fiction, on cheap shock in the works of younger writers. (Yes, you, Dos Passos!) She was fooling herself. Who'd care about these topics? They were the narrow concerns of a woman completely out of step with her time . . . out of sorts with the Percys and McWhinneys . . . the new love of noise in the arts.

How *fresh* the world had seemed years ago! How full of aesthetic possibility when she'd first seen the Puvis de Chavannes frescoes in Paris in . . . what was it, 1902?—and the painter's decorative works in the Boston Public Library five years later. It was the *mood* that mattered in his work, not the contrived situation or subject—a timeless quality, cast always in soft, golden light, transposable from one art form into another. These days, writers knew nothing of painters or vice versa or . . . no. No. That couldn't possibly be true, Willa thought. But writers and painters alike—they were *all* so concerned with gross, easy naturalism, brutalist spectacle.

Could an individual secede, the way a state could remove itself from the union?

She remembered again—she could not forget—sitting with Mrs. Fields and Miss Jewett in the library in the house on Charles Street. The day Miss Jewett told her, "You must know the world before you can know the village!"

But the world was swarming now with ill-behaved children. Wherever they went, they left behind ashpits. No one under forty could appreciate Willa's wisdom, her experiences. Her counsel. No one younger than early middle age could truly believe in death or degeneration. *Youngsters should not even glance at my work.*

Straining, she reached for her dear mother's pen. With her wrapped and wounded hand she scrawled boldly at the top of her outline, *Not Under Forty.*

3

The apartment was far too miserable without Edith's tender presence, so Willa went walking early in the mornings. At Fifth and 23rd she stood admiring the Flatiron in flurries of snow, its blue windows like sketch marks made with a pencil. Women scurried past her, muffled, wrapped, furry as black caterpillars in their coats. Smoke lingered, low over the East River, from the hotel fire.

She sat for a while in what was left of the trellised old building in Central Park where once she'd sipped peaty Chinese tea with Elsie, questioning her about the severity of her war injuries. She wondered how Elsie was faring now in her cottage upriver, in this harsh winter cold.

One day, at the Metropolitan Museum, Willa treated herself to a full half hour gazing at one of her favorite paintings in the city, El Greco's *View of Toledo*. Tufted greens strained as if for succor toward a moistened blue canopy at the top of the canvas. The clouds resembled bushes, the bushes clouds. A ribbon of river knitted together all the compositional elements. Toledo, chalky and scraped-looking, reminded Willa of the cliff dwellings at Mesa Verde. Surely, if Paradise ever existed on Earth, El Greco saw it here (in spite of the harassing presence of the Inquisitor's little men, the worldly gnat horde performing notorious evils, spoiling any Eden). The painting brought to mind a Hebrew phrase Willa had learned from a Jewish friend in her days at *McClure's*: *HaMakom yenahem etkhem*, "The place will comfort you." The word for *place* doubled as the word for *God*, Willa's friend explained—*Mah nora ha-makom he-zeh*, "How awesome is this place."

Willa loved the painting so much she had inserted El Greco into her novel about the archbishop in New Mexico, though the painter had no role in the story. She invented a tale about a New World missionary, passionate about converting the Indians, who had, through a series of fantastical circumstances, carried an El Greco from Valencia to the wilderness known as Albuquerque. This was an implausible detail in the book, insignificant, and yet it guided much of Willa's writing about the Southwest—more than her actual experience of the desert.

When she wrote, "The hills thrust out of the ground so thickly that they seemed to be pushing each other, elbowing each other aside, tipping each other over," she was thinking less of New Mexico than of El Greco's elongated cubes, circles, perpendiculars. It was not that the painter's images provided her with details for the novel; she was not transposing El Greco's Spain onto the American Southwest—not exactly; it was a matter of adopting an aesthetic vision, stirring a potion of colors, shapes, and spiritual delicacy into the rhythms of her sentences.

Poor Elsie. Willa remembered her friend's praise for the accuracy of the landscapes in *Death Comes for the Archbishop*. What would she say if she knew Willa's *real* source? Alas, probably Elsie could never write a novel. She could only grasp the documentary impulse. Reportage. Direct witness. To write about New Mexico, she'd joined political committees and involved herself in Indian affairs. The alchemy of art was beyond her.

At midday Willa lunched at Purcell's, watching, through the big windows, Vs of seagulls twittering in the uneasy skies. Men with bristling brooms swept then salted the sidewalks. Snow folded over the gray bank cornices. Street vendors selling violets out of season (where *did* the flowers come from?) waved the startlingly vivid bouquets. They were wrapped in oiled paper, crackling like ears of corn over a desert fire. As she was leaving the restaurant, Willa heard a Steinway from an upstairs window . . . Bach's "Sheep May Safely Graze." She thought once more of Elsie, with whom she had heard this tune one day, walking with her past an open window, just like this one, shortly after the war. Willa dreamed of how pleasant it would be to offer her cocooned, aching wrist to Elsie, who understood better than anyone the humiliation of infirmity . . . to have Elsie stroke and caress her wound, the way Willa's mother used to rub her scalp whenever she was sick as a child.

Late in the day, Willa caught a bus to the Cloisters, part of a Romanesque Benedictine monastery transported piece by piece to the States from bygone France and reconstructed in upper Manhattan. Always, its atmosphere took her to another time and place, to a world of Dantean order and peace. ("How awesome it is.")

In the Campin Room, standing before a fifteenth-century Altarpiece of the Annunciation, she considered how the altar's religious function transformed every other object in the room, ordinary pieces such as a table, a bench, a basin, a majolica jug, a brass candlestick. In the altar's presence they became ornaments of the Divine. To do that on the page! To make each descriptive element—a couch, a chair, a bone-china dish, a canter of golden white wine—shimmer with divinity.

A fat priest, waddling among other distracted tourists, nodded hello to her. In spite of the godly atmosphere, he appeared out of place here, a loose and lazy man. Like a tropical islander. And that stooped fellow in the corner—she thought she recognized him. He was studying a gilt mirror . . . Wasn't he the "adventurer" she had met in the hospital? Had that man actually existed or was he a hallucinatory figment of her fever that night? Probably this person, now, reminded her of the adventurer because of the green-and-purple rainbow falling across his shoulder. It came from a stained-glass window in the wall, a touch of the Northern Lights in the monastery's enclosed cosmos.

She moved past the altar, through an arched stone doorway into a room of marble sarcophagi.

That night, back in her apartment, sipping chicken noodle soup to line her stomach against the unsettling effects of the pain pills, she glimpsed the phrase she had scribbled on her outline, *Not Under Forty*. She smiled with contentment. I may be old and out of step, she thought, raising her eyes to her bookshelf, but I am strengthened by my hard-won tactics. Compression. Precision. Transubstantiation. The alchemy of art.

4

"The Spiritual Problem of Modern Man."

What was Elsie up to? "Dearest Willa: Years ago, when I was living in my hut, I was so grateful for the Gauguin book you sent me. It kept me company during those rough first nights." This was the note slipped into the article by Carl Jung Elsie had just sent.

Gauguin? Surely not! Willa would never have championed such a pagan. The naked brown women. The lack of depth and perspective. Elsie must be mistaken.

"Now, as you recover from your injury, allow me to return the favor. You know the high regard in which I have always held Dr. Jung. Here is a piece he has written drawing upon some of his experiences in the Southwest, decades ago. May you find wisdom and comfort in it."

Irritated, Willa shifted in her desk chair. Elsie knew how little patience she had for psychological twaddle. The last thing she needed was wisdom. What she required was someone to remove this infernal cast. (Curse her metal thumb!) A strong cocktail wouldn't hurt either.

Ah. Now Elsie came to the point: "Have you seen the 'Portable' editions that Viking has published lately—compendia of various writers' works, overviews of their literary careers? An agent has approached me, by letter, about putting together a 'Portable Cather.' I wondered if you would ever consider such an undertaking."

Oh, that desperate girl, always hustling!

Last year, Elsie had proposed a critical study of the poetry of Robert Frost. The year before that, it was another book about the Indians . . . well, she *was* living paycheck to paycheck, project to project, but still . . . she tossed ideas like darts into the world, hoping one would stick.

"The agent, a man named Silas McWhinney, an acquaintance of yours, I believe . . ."

Groaning, Willa reached for her pen:

"I could never be persuaded to submit to a 'Portable Cather.' These 'Portables' seem to be the last derivative of the torrent of anthologies which very nearly wiped out all the dignity and nearly all the profits of the legitimate publishing business. Everybody wants to 'get by' easy, schools, teachers, and pupils. Nobody wants to toil through *For Whom the Bell Tolls* when they can read the worst chapters of the book and say 'Hemingway? Oh, yes, sure!' Why are you willing to squander your time and scatter your attention for a miserable collection that means to get by as a 'Portable'? Such a waste of energy! Let me wish you happy days and good luck on some new book that might actually engage you and ask that you forget this insidious 'Portable' suggestion."

Elsie's note ended with an invitation to come stay with her in her cottage at Sneden's Landing. At the moment, nothing sounded less appealing to Willa than sitting in some mildewed room by a clamorous river listening to Elsie's money troubles.

Willa's angry reply had sapped the feeling in her hand . . . sapped her will to live . . . my *god*, what she'd give for one of Edith's dry martinis.

Not Sneden's Landing. But maybe a trip *somewhere*, to escape the loneliness of the apartment until Edith's return. Iceland? An adventure!

No. *Imaginary* adventures were about all she could manage right now.

It wasn't the right season; the weather would be a challenge . . . but she *could* take a train and then a ferry to Grand Manan, spend a few days roughing out an essay . . .

Where *was* Edith now? Willa sorted through the postcards. The beaches near Barcelona. Franco. Fascists. Falangists.

The worldly gnat horde.

Come home, Edith!

Willa closed her eyes. She imagined staying in a comfortable boarding house in Paris at the time of Henry Adams, glancing out her window to see the dapper old gent prowling around the candlelit cathedral . . . ah, but *that* Europe was long gone . . . even the Europe of Gertrude Stein, whom Willa could never stand—all those lazy young poseurs in the "salon" gathered at the feet of that silly, pompous woman . . . horrible Cubists crowding the walls—even *those* days had frittered away like a red silk scarf on the wind.

Self-pity. Willa wondered if she had let it leak into her letters to Edith. If unscrupulous snakes such as Silas McWhinney were already slithering about, nosing around for collectibles, what would stop them from publishing Willa's letters after she was gone? What would be worse, the world's grotesque curiosity pawing through her sentences, scrabbling for clues to her "private life," her nights with Isabelle, with Edith . . . "None of your damn business!" Willa said aloud. She could not abide the laying bare of emotional storms, anger, self-loathing, bitterness . . .

Best to retrieve her correspondence from her friends. Burn the letters. A self-immolation. Leave nothing behind in this wretched wasteland.

She reread the letter she had just dashed off to Elsie. What would a dispassionate observer say about it? Perhaps she was being too hard on the girl. (She still thought of Elsie as a girl!) A hard-luck case, to be sure. Not without talent, but for some reason she had never found her artistic center. Always discontented. She had published those pieces in *Harper's* about how fulfilling it had been, a life-changing renewal, to remodel the mud hut in Tesuque. She'd said she could never return to New England after spending a "summer night on a cliff of the Ancient People," listening to an "old Indian burst into rhythmic chant." (How *did* her editors let her get away with such resounding clichés?) She wrote Willa letters— how rapturous it was, lighting fires of gnarled roots on a gray rock ledge beneath the autumn sky. Dr. Jung's insights had taught her the importance of "claiming one's rights in the primeval kingdom of the earth," she said. The Southwestern desert was the ideal spot for her to stake her claim.

But then, after only two years living in the hut, two harsh winters, she experienced what she later described to Willa as a "norther," an unexpected chilling breeze blowing through her bones one day as she was riding a horse from Santa Fe to Tesuque over shell-pink sand hills. It was early spring; the winter had been cold, brazenly so, but not enough snow had fallen to feed the Tesuque River. Its bed was nearly dry. The cottonwoods remained mostly bare, shivering in a combustible wind. Elsie's throat squeezed with a sudden, massive thirst and the realization rippled through her body, her brain, *This is not my country.*

Within a month she was laid up, a pale, thin wreck in a friend's back bedroom in an apartment on 10th Street. Then she made her move to Sneden's Landing. Willa had always assumed that extreme weather and unsteady magazine assignments had accounted for Elsie's "norther." She *did* return to New Mexico, briefly, in the early 1930s, when FDR appointed a man named John Collier, one of her old activists-in-arms along with those silly Bryn Mawr ladies, to the post of Indian Commissioner. Collier had asked Elsie to write a series of economic and social-condition reports on Pueblo communities for the Department of the Interior. Then the money for *that* project dried up as well.

Elsie returned to her cottage on the Hudson. Occasionally, she would catch a train into Manhattan. She and Willa would meet for tea. After one such afternoon, an awkward meeting stippled with silences (Elsie had been on one of her Dr. Jung kicks, and Willa was having none of it), Elsie wrote Willa a letter: the "freshness of heart and intense enthusiasm for life" she had first known in Willa "seemed buried deep below the surface these days." Conversations were hard with her now, Elsie said, always "preceded by a sort of creaking of the machinery, characterized by blocks and sudden breaks that sometimes sweep you on." She hoped Willa was not withdrawing from her friends. She wished her old companion health, peace, and happiness.

They had seen little of each other since then.

Now Elsie had popped up again, having heard of Willa's mishap. She expressed renewed concern for Willa's mental outlook. Well. Willa set aside her reply to the girl. She picked up Dr. Jung. Spiritual problems, indeed. He mentioned a "Pueblo Elder" he had met years ago in Santa Fe, Ochwiay Bianco. The chieftain had taught him how European man must extricate himself from the "cloud of his own moral incense" and embrace the more natural, more expansive cosmos of peoples living in harmony with the Earth. (Gauguin and his island nymphs!) "Modern man has lost all the metaphysical certainties of his medieval brother, and set up in their place the ideals of material security, general welfare, and humanitarianism," Willa read. Hard to disagree. She recalled the medieval serenity of the Cloisters. "But security has gone by the wayside. We have begun to see that every step forward in material 'progress' steadily increases the threat of global catastrophe. The imagination shrinks in terror from such a picture." Yes, Willa thought. But—this is supposed to comfort me? She imagined Edith sunning at the Costa Brava . . . moist, warm rocks . . . Franco's tanks grinding away on the horizon. "The upheaval of the world and the upheaval of our consciousness are one and the same," Jung wrote. Irritably, Willa flung the papers aside.

The piles remained on her floor for days, a lingering reproach from Elsie, her oh-so-annoying friend; it hurt too much to bend and pick them up.

5

"The world broke in two in 1922 or thereabouts, and the persons and prejudices in these sketches slid back into yesterday's seven thousand years," Willa wrote painfully on her manuscript beneath the title *Not Under Forty*. "It is for the backward, and by one of their number, that these sketches were written."

She had discarded the essays on narrative and shock in modern novels. Instead, she had decided to concentrate on her memories of literary people and occasions. The beautiful past: a favorite, well-worn cushion to lean on. She squeezed her wrist beneath the leather sheath. Her skin itched inside the cast. She picked up her mother's pen. She wrote: "One morning when the cantaloupes were particularly fine, Mrs. Fields began to tell me of Henry James's father..."

What an innocent she had been when she first visited Charles Street! You did not go there to hear about the past, but to step into it, to be absorbed into a protective and cherished sanctuary against the pile-driving present. Upon entering the small reception area and climbing the thickly carpeted stairway into the drawing room, whose back windows oversaw a lush green garden, Willa always feared she'd say something foolish and embarrass herself in front of the magnificent ladies. She recalled walking into the room one morning, Miss Jewett puffing up her full figure, her body a halo of gray, asking Willa what she thought of Manet and the Impressionists. "Have you ever heard of such a thing as blue snow or a man's black hat turning purple in the sun?" Willa didn't know what to say.

Or the day Mrs. Fields recited Milton: "in luxurious cities . . . the noise / Of riot ascends above their loftiest towers, / And injury and outrage." Willa observed how well the poet's imagery evoked the tumult of Babylon and Rome. "And New York," quipped Mrs. Fields. Willa blushed at her own girlish solemnity.

On another occasion, Mrs. Fields, slight and fragile, adjusting the Venetian lace on her hair, muttered, at random, an obscure line of poetry, "A bracelet of bright hair about the bone." Shyly, Willa confessed she didn't recognize those very nice words. "Surely, that would be Dr. Donne," said Mrs. Fields, and without a by-your-leave she pulled from the library shelves two ponderous volumes of John Donne's verse for Willa to "peruse" at her leisure.

Nothing but ghosts now, Miss Jewett and Mrs. Fields, these dear, sweet guardians of language, grace, dignity. Willa closed her eyes. It was too painful, just at the moment, to approach, in memory, the gentle slope of Charles Street.

So she sailed her thoughts forward to another spectacular old woman she'd met, on her last, sad trip to Europe just after the war. Each evening that summer at Aix-les-Bains, in the dining room of the Grand-Hotel d'Aix, overlooking a tiny plaza notable for its bronze head of Queen Victoria, Willa would see a fine elderly woman whose head might have been a marble bust, it was so gorgeously shaped. Forehead low and straight. Her hips had absorbed the stoutness of age, but she carried herself with delicacy. A slight odor of spring-washed violets rose from the creases of her sleeves. One night a group of diners sat discussing the "unfortunate Soviet experiment in Russia." When the boisterous party had left, Willa, seated alone at a table near the center of the room, glanced at the old woman, who was finishing her coffee and dessert. Her bearing reminded Willa of Miss Jewett; perhaps that's why Willa took a chance. She said, "It's fortunate that the great group of Russian writers—Gogol, Tolstoy, Turgenev—didn't live to see the Revolution."

"Yes." The lady sighed. "For Turgenev, especially, all this would have been very terrible. I knew him well at one time."

Startled, Willa studied the woman's face more closely, the papery skin pancaked with powder.

"I saw him very often when I was a young girl. I was much interested in German, in the great works. I was making a translation of *Faust*, for my own pleasure, merely, and Turgenev used to go over my translation and correct it. He was a great friend of my uncle. I was brought up in my uncle's house, you see."

"And who was your uncle?" Willa asked.

"A man of letters, Gustave Flaubert, you may perhaps know . . ."

Willa was so instantly and profoundly moved by this chance encounter—the two of them isolated in Europe's splendid ruins— she rose from her chair, lifted one of the woman's lovely hands, and kissed it.

"Oh, that is not necessary! That is not at all necessary," the woman exclaimed, embarrassed.

"In homage to a great period," Willa murmured, her eyes brimming with tears. "To the names that make both our voices tremble."

The woman laughed and laughed, delighted.

Willa teared up again, seated at her desk. Ghosts. Nothing but ephemera. Snow whispered against her window. The past *was* beautiful . . . for that reason, it would be harder to revisit than she'd thought.

6

Under heavy snowfall, which prevented a preponderance of motor cars on the streets, the city appeared to belong to an earlier century, prior to world wars and the deaths of dozens in hotel infernos. It was again a city of horse-drawn carriages moving lazily beneath lavender shadows along the tree-lined edges of Central Park. Willa could imagine a Schubert lieder issuing from the throbbing yellow parlors of Midtown music halls—*Winterreise* or "Der Doppelganger" from *Swan's Song*: "Still is the night. / The streets are at rest. / Here is the house where my loved one lived; / Long it is, since she left town."

Edith, come home!

Willa remembered fondly, as a young woman in Pittsburgh, first hearing Wagner's *Tannhäuser*. Isabelle had taken her to an afternoon matinee. The singers were so beset with head colds, common in winter in that foggy river town, their arias were moistened with coughs. But such was the power of Wagner, not even crumbling human voices could tarnish his timelessness.

Willa heard now, from up the street as she stood on the icy sidewalk, a bawdy saloon song, delivered terribly but with genuinely moving conviction by an alcoholic diva. It obviously cost the crack-voiced singer something to offer such a convincing performance of her blues, just as her listeners also bled, no doubt. And maybe this *was* the day's proper accompaniment, given the increasingly sordid news out of Europe, the cancer spreading from Spain, France's surrender to the Germans . . . Leave it to Edith to choose this moment to travel alone, curious, blithely ignoring the dangers . . .

An adventurer, bless her. Like Elsie. Well. Bless her, too. Damn her stubbornness.

"The War to End All Wars" seemed to have been mere practice for bloodthirsty men, the planet's nastiest creatures. The grief Willa felt for the world—a fragile snow globe—she no longer had the spiritual resources to counter.

In the distance, the Grace Church bell, faint, like the tinkling of a child's sleigh. Willa recalled all the snows of yesteryear on the flat, Western plains.

She took a slow step. To aid with her footing today, she relied on the cane Elsie had sent her. An odd object: more than just functional . . . ceremonial, somehow . . . well, it *had* been the gift of a priest, hadn't it? Elsie had mentioned its resemblance to a Pueblo "power stick." Willa was almost convinced that if she waved the cane properly, she could halt this cascading storm. But she lacked any knowledge of magic. To her fellow strollers, she was just another old woman wielding an ancient walking stick, a cast wrapped tightly around her arm.

Gazing at her smeary face in a shop window, she recalled one of the essays she had recently abandoned: *How does a writer know where to start a novel? Or the story of someone's life?* If you present a character chronologically, securing the reader's sympathy during a tragic or generous youth, you can mitigate that character's future bad behavior. The fine first impression will never quite dissipate, and the reader will forgive the character anything: cranky illness, growing desperation, or greed. Conversely—Willa gripped the cane more firmly—if we meet a character in puling old age, spitting at others in misanthropic rage, no amount of youthful exuberance, revisited through narrative time travel, can erase the painful introduction.

Willa imagined her fellow citizens' notions of *her*: a withered badger in her fancy fox fur coat, snooty, angry, not to be trifled with . . .

Not far off the mark.

Oh, but my laughter *did* once tickle the tops of bare Midwestern trees . . . my sleigh sliding along downy, wet furrows of snow!

Which Willa am I?

Flakes dripped from the awnings, moistening her face, blurring her vision. In the store window, the reflection of her features gave way to sharpening definitions of objects on the other side of the glass, as if the objects were asserting their permanence over her fleeting presence on Earth. Musical instruments. A trombone, a bassoon. A scratched yellow oud. A Steinway piano. A young customer sat there on a plush leather stool, playing a Scott Joplin rag. Through the weather-slapped window, the keyboard resembled a long white brushstroke, as in an Impressionist painting. From behind Willa, the street scene captured in the glass—one or two parked cars, shoppers standing by the curb holding bags—appeared static, a framed tableau on a canvas. The music roamed through several time signatures, past, present, future folded into a single minor phrase. The contrast, like the swirling snow, dizzied Willa. She turned, lost control of the cane, and slipped on the frozen concrete.

A lance of pain at the top of her hip.

Smoke clotted, black, above the East River.

She thought she saw, in the passing crowd, a tall Native man wearing a hard hat. Faces jostled above her.

"Oh my! Lady, lady, are you all right?" someone said.

"Yes, yes . . ."

Geese floated against the snow-laden clouds like blue shadows cast by a child's hands across a candlelit wall.

A woman helped her up. Handed her the cane. Was this the sort of pain Elsie always endured, ever since the war? How could she possibly manage? "Thank you, thank you," Willa said. Then, once more, she was alone, standing unsteadily in front of the music store window. The briefness of kindness in the city. The last selfless gestures in a world of endless battles . . .

She made up her mind: she would escape to Grand Manan.

7

She'd been fine until she'd met the young geologist on the ferry (an ancient scow that *had* to be one of the worst steamships in America). "Fine" was too strong a word, perhaps. Her wrist still ached whenever the air turned chilly, as it did every day. Her hip was sore from the spill she'd taken on the sidewalk, a big blue bruise. When the train had pulled out of Port Authority, heading north into the scoured outer boroughs, past wind-blasted family structures made of clapboard, uninsulated, tattered, exposed to Canadian northers and smoke from inefficient factories, she'd slipped into a funk. From her place in the coach—a cast-off car from a defunct railroad once traveling out of Boston, seat backs flaking into grime, gummy and torn—she could see Manhattan receding, its island nature clearly on display. It looked vulnerable and lonely. The river appeared to be stricken, still, with the ashen aftermath of the hotel fire, though this hardly seemed possible. Perhaps she perceived, through some strange second sight, a moral malaise hanging over the city like a hatch of hungry insects on the plains. All the Native men and women, all the slaves, we'd slaughtered here to develop this narrow jut of land . . . now we were slaughtering ourselves, out of a surfeit of carelessness and greed.

Lord. If she didn't restrain herself, she'd turn into Elsie or her soft-headed doctor, Mr. Jung: strident idealists, God save us all.

Once the train angled east, toward sunrise and the sea, she began to relax. She was going to another island, but Grand Manan never felt lonely. Already, she could almost breathe the cozy, glowing pine smell of the brick fireplace in her cottage; she was able to sleep in spite of the train's clangorous bucking.

Then, later, that smug young man on the ferry unsettled her. No, to be fair, he wasn't smug. In truth, he'd behaved rather graciously. It was his certainty about the planet that caused Willa so much damned discomfort.

She'd been standing on the ferry deck watching fishermen check their herring weirs. Wiry fellows wearing oilcloth suits stood on the muddy shore, spreading nets along a series of wooden stakes planted in a shallow cove. A young man joined her at the railing. He was tall and thin, red-haired with a prominent Adam's apple and pale skin patchy with irritation, scattered like strawberry juice on his face and neck. "Fascinating, isn't it?" he said.

"Yes," Willa agreed.

"So the herring will bump into the fence—that line of stakes, there—and be directed into the weir?"

"Yes, I think that's the way it works," Willa said.

The young man nodded. "I've heard this method is based on old Native practices. Their hooks and spears didn't work, you know, so they devised traps of sticks with branches and bushes woven in between."

Willa smiled in a tight, dismissive way she hoped would persuade him to leave her alone.

"Excuse me, but . . . are you Willa Cather?" he asked.

"I am." Warily.

"I recognized you from newspaper pictures. Forgive me for bothering you . . . your novel, *The Professor's House* . . . it's one of my favorites."

"Thank you." She smiled more generously now.

"Maybe because *I'm* a professor." He grinned like a boy. "You got the details just right. The college town atmosphere. The pinched academic politics."

"That pleases me. Where do you teach?"

"Connecticut. A tiny private school. You wouldn't have heard of it."

"Historian? Native customs?"

Chapter 7

"No. Actually, I'm a geologist. You're going to Grand Manan?"

"As a matter of fact."

"It's my primary research site. Intriguing place."

"It's certainly beautiful. Why does it intrigue you so much?"

"Oh, it's got what you might call a . . . I don't know . . . a split personality, I suppose."

"I don't understand."

Shy but eager, he explained, "Well, the island's western half . . . recently, we've discovered its base. It consists of Late Triassic lava. The eastern side—it was made from metamorphosed sedimentary rock, much older than the younger basalts in the west. These two halves of the island—they must have been forced together by ice. Glacial movement. Erosion."

Willa pondered this information, frowning, watching silver fish flash inside the seines. "And so . . . the oldest segments of the island . . . about how many centuries would you say . . ."

"A hundred and thirty-six million years. Roughly," the young man answered.

They exchanged a few more pleasantries, he wished her well with her writing, and the encounter ended. It wasn't until that night, after a leisurely dinner at Tatton's Corner (lamb chops, mint chutney), a fine carafe of wine imported from Saint John's, and a nice fire in her Whale Cove cottage—while a cool, soft rain pattered the thin wooden eaves—that she turned surly, too restless to sleep. A hundred and thirty-six million years! Who could possibly bear the weight of such an eternity? Certainly not her. With her tottery hip! She loved the island because each time she arrived here she felt she was discovering it anew, the blue spruce forests, the ponds, the birches and the swaying black alders, the bushy rowan trees. It was always as if, on her first morning back, the landscape had assembled itself freshly, just for her. But now this geologist, this arrogant young professor with his numbers and his rock strata, he had cast her into the cauldron of infinity, world without end, when already she'd lived long enough to see most of what she cared about in the world, most of the people she'd loved, end—most definitively. He had mocked her little hours, her limited capacity for endurance.

Cruel, crude existence. Why was she even still here?

The morning sun through the cottage windows renewed her somewhat: dazzling and direct, like the light at Mesa Verde years ago. The purplish cast of the cliffs there, the yellow of the turning aspens in the fall, and the leathery leaves of the red sumac combined to wash the great Southwestern sky with earthen tints, as if the firmament were a giant hanging garden rich with mineral soil.

She rose, wrapped herself in an eiderdown bathrobe, poked the embers in her fireplace briefly back to life, and splashed her face at her walnut washstand. She stood for a while in her doorway, sipping black coffee, inhaling the brisk salt air. A snowshoe hare bounded past her, searching for last summer's vanished clover, no doubt; the familiar landmarks, the yellow toadstools, the white mushrooms, were also gone. "Try again in a few months, little fellow," Willa said, her breath a fleeting mist.

Midmorning, she donned a flannel shirt and a leather coat, and she took a walk through the bare spruce woods, past an old, forked tree struck by lightning, Willa surmised, its shallow roots like a nest of sightless worms emerging from the dirt. An odor evoking roasting acorns rode the air. It dissipated beneath another wave of sea salt on an icy westerly breeze. She wished she'd brought Elsie's cane to help her get about. She'd left it in the cottage.

Her sore body, its bruises and scars like map lines inscribed in the skin of a bison from her old Nebraska plains . . . directions to an undetermined landscape . . .

She came to a narrow sandstone cliff, a crumbling reddish drop two hundred feet into the ocean. Gulls circled silver waves, foam skirting the island like lace. In the east, the sky darkened, El Greco green. She wondered if she was far enough north to see the Aurora Borealis. "A lazy adventurer," she said aloud, her words a curl of smoke. "That's me."

(Briefly, she recalled dancing in the desert to the chiming of a Mexican guitar, a vital young woman, ready to go anywhere—a lifetime ago! Which Willa am I?)

She found a smooth outcrop to sit on, facing the sea. Young or old, this stone? Moist, brown, crusted with brittle lichen branching like the arteries bluing the back of her hand. Her companion from the ferry, the rough-skinned scientist—probably he was hopping about nearby, measuring, calculating, diminishing her importance on this rock.

In her novel, the one he'd liked so much, she had contrasted the brooding, self-absorbed scholar in his study with a young adventurer, boldly exploring the Southwest's Native dwellings.

My god, she thought. My god. Of course.

It hit her in the muscles of her heart, like lightning striking the trunk of the tree: *I* am the inert professor in that book, aren't I? Reliving the *idea* of New Mexico in my mind rather than revisiting it regularly.

And if *that* was true—dare she admit it?—Elsie Sergeant was the young adventurer, the one who'd actually moved there to establish residence, however briefly. The sedentary man of texts versus the desert activist. *Really*—was that the gist of her novel? Lord, thought Willa. Elsie and me? The possibility startled her like a taste of snow on her tongue.

She'd gotten cold, sitting so still. She tried to rise, wished again for the cane.

All these years . . . Elsie as Willa's Muse, the disturbing, enabling force moving the pen in her hand? *Could* it be so? And oh, how was the poor girl faring now . . . that poor, heedless girl?

In her inertia, Willa had become neglectful, just as she had gotten careless with Edith.

She watched the sea fold into itself, then fold and fold again.

Following a fitful nap in the early afternoon, as light rain tittered among the remaining leaves in the woods, clinging, stubborn and dead, to frosted limbs, Willa walked again, just to stir the blood. This time she took Elsie's cane to navigate mud slopes, snowmelts, crevices pelted with slick brown moss. The cane left mucky holes in the earth. She poked about like an old-fashioned Irish potato farmer. Or a grave digger, Willa thought.

She'd awakened from her sleep thinking of Elsie. If all stories started with *trouble*, as Willa believed they did—some question demanding to be answered—then certainly Elsie had been a constant inspiration for Willa. That girl was nothing *but* trouble! Always arguing about the purpose of art, insisting upon writing's social utility, its didactic function, ignoring the aesthetic impulse, the drive toward timelessness.

Why Elsie's effect on her work suddenly seemed clearer to her now, she didn't know. The young scientist on the boat, perhaps, mentioning *The Professor's House*; the cane; adventurers (real and imaginary) . . .

In any case, now that Willa considered the matter, she believed, with chagrin, that many of her books must have enacted her tensions with Elsie. It seemed hard to deny. Over and over, Willa had pitted feeling against thinking, action against passivity. Ivy Peters/Neil Herbert; Father Vaillant/ Father Latour: her cherished characters always came down to two.

Willa and Elsie.

Was that true?

And: Who emerged from the struggle unscathed?

This sounded Jungian. Willa laughed, poking the ground with the cane.

What was it Elsie had written in her letter, going on and on about the priest who'd offered her the stick? Something like, "The flaws in his character allowed the light of his soul to shine, like chinks in an old adobe wall letting in the sun." Her tedious idealism! Well. Perhaps there *was* some wisdom in it, some clue to understanding Elsie.

Understanding us all.

Willa raised the power stick, pumped it skyward. Nothing happened. Of course. No thunder, no instant squall. No feathery plummet of big gray geese, dying in droves.

As Willa had told Elsie many times, the artist controlled only her private material.

Willa dined that evening at the Rose, down the hill from her cottage. Beet salad, Atlantic salmon, brussels sprouts. A mild Chardonnay. The mellow, candlelit atmosphere, the slow and gentle pace of the wait staff, made her realize how upset she'd been, this afternoon, with Elsie. Really, she surprised herself. Naturally, the truth about her work was that every contrast she'd sketched revealed the ambivalence in her *own* nature. If anything, Elsie had simply made the contradictions more apparent by acting out, over the years, certain traits Willa lacked the courage to indulge. In this regard, Elsie had been good for her.

A good and valued friend.

And now, oh . . . one of the servers in the restaurant, a dark-haired girl, maybe twenty, reminded Willa of daguerreotypes she'd seen of her mother as a child. Willa trembled. She feared she'd lose control. As an old woman, declining rapidly after a stroke, her mother had resembled nothing so much as a soiled hospital bedsheet, but at the very end of her life, within hours of her passing, her eyes came clear. Once more, they projected the vivid blue depths of childhood. Was she really seeing an earlier world? Willa thought so at the time. She poured a second glass of wine. In spite of herself, she wept.

The Rose's manager, a tiny, garrulous man whose name Willa could never remember, though she'd become fond of him over many visits to the island, approached her table warmly. He asked after her health ("Your arm! It's not badly hurt?") and told her if she needed anything, to please let him know. She wiped her eyes with her napkin. She thanked him.

"It's a shaky time," he said. "We must all stick together."

"What do you mean?" Willa asked.

He told her he'd lately heard rumors that German submarines had been spotted off the coast of Grand Manan. "This war business in Europe . . . let's hope it doesn't find its way over here, eh? Let's hope the world can be saved."

"Amen," Willa murmured.

He topped off her glass before making his way to another table to greet a laughing new flurry of diners.

In the middle of the night she woke from a dream of her mother's eyes—vast blue seas into which she was sorely tempted to dive—to discover black smoke choking the life out of her.

She half rose in bed. Through her bedroom doorway she glimpsed a chunk of log singeing the carpet on the granite floor in front of the fireplace. Apparently, she had pulled the carpet too close to the logs before going to sleep. (She'd been sitting on the carpet, near the fire.) The wood had popped from the grate.

Flames burst from the wool's rumpled edge. Willa sank into the sweaty cleft of her pillow. She felt profoundly weary. She remembered the smell of charred flesh in the emergency room at French Hospital. All right . . . all right, she thought, why not . . . to dissolve, to *give* yourself to something bigger . . .

She closed her eyes, swam partway into sleep. *So this is how you die.*

Midmorning. She knew she should stay inside. She should rough out an essay, make some use of this trip, but an odor of ash remained in the place, her coffee had gone cold, her head ached, and she had difficulty concentrating. She put on her heavy shirt and her coat.

Somehow, last night, she had stirred herself: some primitive impulse to live. The midnight reptilian brain. She'd stumbled to the door. Grabbed the carpet and dragged it out into the downpour.

Now, on a moist hillock overlooking the cottage, gazing out at the ocean's silver-blue curvature, she recalled her mother's tender eyes. She wondered if submarines clotted the seabed, like a form of insidious plankton poisoning the waters. She wished she could raise a barrier around the island.

It was creeping too close. All of it.

The sun made a sizzling yolk, trembling at the red-fogged edge of the sea.

Using Elsie's cane for leverage, Willa climbed higher, as close to the sky as she could get. "Lift me up! Let me off!" she called to the purple clouds. She could see, far below, at the northwest head of the island, facing the Bay of Fundy, the lighthouse at Long Eddy Point. Legends said the station's first engineer, in 1857 or so, discovered the sole survivor of the wreck of the *Lord Ashburton* shivering in a barn. It was said that, ever since, the perished souls of the fellow's shipmates powered the station's light.

She turned toward the woods. A barbed-wire fence ringed a house and barn nearby, on the eastern slope of the hill. She'd never noticed fences on this island. Was this a new development? A sign of increasing mistrust among the neighbors?

How had we gone from offering warm illumination to walling ourselves off from one another?

She laughed aloud: bursts of frosty smoke. She sounded like Elsie again. Well, after all, the girl wasn't always wrong, Willa thought, clutching the cane. Probably, I haven't been fair to her. Yes, she was an irritating idealist, but just like Willa's cousin in the gun smoke of France, Elsie had, on occasion, genuinely sacrificed herself for others.

Willa's own books told the tale, didn't they? On balance, the active characters, the adventurers, were far more pleasing than the passive ones. The world needed saving, and it wasn't the Willas that would do it.

Perhaps she should invite Elsie down to the apartment for Christmas. She hadn't seen her in such a long time. Edith liked her well enough. Willa could dust the Pueblo pottery on the mantelpiece, make sure it caught the sun . . . Elsie would be so pleased . . .

In a streak of sun glare on the sea, just beyond the bay, a black object bobbed among the waves. Willa couldn't make it out. Her spine went cold. A submarine? No. Too large. A ship? A barge? A plume of smoke, like a ball of twine unwinding, hovered in the air. Whatever it was, it seemed to be drifting. In trouble. Willa was no nautical captain, but . . . those movements *were* erratic, weren't they?

The lighthouse sent out its beam, but no one could see it from this distance in the daylight. The weak pulse of dead souls.

Whatever would happen in the next few moments, Willa— useless arm, weakened hip—was the event's only witness, standing high above the water. She was as helpless as she'd been on the boat the night of the hotel fire.

Last night's dream came to her again. Her mother's eyes. Vast. Inviting.

"Oh, Elsie," Willa whispered, turning away, into the woods' green shadows. Her breath bloomed and then it vanished. "The world . . . with all its terrible wounds . . . it can't be saved."

Book Three

Boston, 1908

Willa and Elsie stood a mere seven steps from the seven-tiered stoop of the house on Charles Street. Willa stopped her friend by the curb. Time always seemed to bend for her just before she entered this place, the past washing over the present like a wave, slowing and quickening all at once, a series of instants, some frozen, some gone forever.

Both women were vibrant, bouncy, and eager. Elsie had arrived in Boston last night, on a train from New York, just to visit this fabled old house in her friend's company.

"I very much want you to meet Miss Jewett and Mrs. Fields." Willa had been saying this for months as she sat with Elsie in the offices of *McClure's* magazine. "They changed my life and they may change yours."

Now she said, "Before we go inside, Elsie, let me ask you something."

"Of course. What is it?"

Willa buttoned her mauve wool jacket and adjusted the feathered felt hat on her head. "I want to know if you're serious."

"What about?"

"Art."

Elsie laughed.

"I mean it."

"Willa! You're so solemn!"

"This *is* a solemn matter. Especially for our hosts."

"Well, I mean, *I* don't know. Honestly . . ."

Willa sighed. She pointed at the massive black door; above it, the number 148 in gold plating fastened to the lintel. "Do you know . . .

the world's finest literary minds have passed through there? Dickens, Carlyle, Thackeray . . ."

"I certainly don't belong in their company," Elsie said.

"Neither do I. But these ladies . . . they've preserved in here . . . it's like a greenhouse . . . I don't know how to put it . . . they've maintained something like the *essence* of literary ambition . . . it's in the very walls of the place."

"Yes. I think I understand."

"It's important to them that we try to be worthy . . . like the people they've entertained in the past."

"Yes, ma'am!" Primly, Elsie straightened the hem of her sweater.

"Elsie, please don't embarrass me."

"I won't. I'm grateful you asked me to come. It's just that . . . Willa, you make it sound like a wax museum."

"They cherish tradition."

"Okay, fine, but . . ."

"I'm talking about—"

"I know, Willa. I know what you're talking about. It's all right. I won't mortify you. Promise."

"You *have* told me writing is important to you."

"Yes. Of course it is!"

"So then . . . what do you want to *do* with it?"

"Do?"

"They'll want to know."

"Our inquisitors?"

"Our *hosts*! I'm trying to prepare you—"

"What do you want me to say? I'm struggling to be an artist? Is that it?"

"Well . . ."

"Willa, really, do people *think* of themselves that way? Seriously? Do you?"

"Yes."

Elsie laughed again, softly this time. "I'm sure you do. And why not? Your stories have earned you the right."

"That's what I'm trying to tell you, Elsie. These ladies have taught me . . . well, to respect myself. Don't laugh. It's the God's truth."

"Dear. You're an idealist."

"There's nothing wrong with ambition."

"No. But there are other ways to approach it."

"Like what?"

"Like reporting."

"Oh pooh. So we're back to your reformist nonsense? 'In six months, we can clean up the tenements, tear down all the fire traps!'"

"Well, yes! We can do a lot of good, Willa. Writing speeches. Narrating newsreels. Documenting the obscure little wars in—"

"War! Elsie! My poor girl . . ."

"Anyway. Anyway. Willa, I'm sorry. These are your special friends. I want this to be a splendid afternoon for you. So. Tell me what to say."

"Elsie, I swear . . ."

"Go on. If I'm supposed to be an *artiste*, then . . . how do I present myself?"

Willa studied her face. "You mean it? Will you listen to me? Just this once?"

"Absolutely."

"Well, okay, to begin with . . ."

"Yes?"

"If the talk turns to novels, which it probably will . . ."

"All right . . ."

" You might distinguish between forms of amusement and aesthetic objects," Willa said. "The latter is our goal, of course. Mrs. Fields believes young writers, in the early stages of their careers . . ."

"Like you and me?" Elsie interjected. "Young and bold! Full of promise!"

Willa nodded impatiently. "Naturally, we tend to be effusive, testing our limits. Too much ornamentation, overstuffed plots . . ."

"My god, is this *really* what conversation is like in that house?"

"It is. I've heard Mrs. Fields say this many times, Elsie, and I guarantee, it would endear you to her if you were to address it: something along the lines of . . . well, you might argue that maturity in an artist shows itself in greater compression, refinement, sharper precision . . ."

"You *really* want me to say that?"

"Or . . ."

"How about this?" Elsie lifted the hem of her sweater; it barely covered her midriff. "Look, ladies, like our outfits, our sentences get shorter and shorter and shorter!"

"You're incorrigible!" Willa said.

Willa said, "Before we take another step, remember: Miss Jewett is the short, plump one, the slightly older woman, gray. Mrs. Fields is slender, paler, more delicate in her tastes."

Elsie nodded.

"She tends to reminisce about Dickens. The past is still alive for her. Her life is like a series of snapshots, all neatly framed and sitting on the mantel. Miss Jewett, despite her love of tradition, is very much *present*, aware of younger writers . . . mostly, I have to say, in a negative sense . . ."

"It seems they're very different," Elsie said.

"Yes," Willa replied. "I suppose, in many ways, they *are* an odd pair."

Elsie smiled at her friend.

Willa said, "Do you remember that scene in Dante . . . the poor pilgrim comes to the Gate of Purgatory—the sacred realm, you know, where souls are assured of not being damned?"

"No. I'm ashamed to say I've never read it."

"Well, Dante has to climb three steps to be admitted. The first is carved from clear white marble, reflecting his face; the second is deep purple, cracked, made of roughened stone; the third's 'as flaming red / as blood that spurts from a vein.'"

Elsie shook her head.

"It's an allegory," Willa said. "The path to absolution: seeing one-self clearly, recognizing one's cracked and broken state and, finally, accepting grace." She stood at the foot of the stoop. "Always, before mounting these steps, I think of that passage. I imagine myself as the pilgrim."

Elsie laughed.

"*Now* what's funny?"

"Honestly. You amaze me. I've never met anyone like you."

"I should hope not!"

"Really, Willa. Most people . . . they speak of art, how it's enriched their lives or offered them a short break from trouble. But you . . . it's like . . . it's like . . . you're *breathing* art. The paint, the backstage dust, the ink."

Willa straightened her hat. "And what's so astonishing about that?"

"Well . . . it's just . . . art's place . . . I don't know . . . the world isn't so simple, is it?"

"Nonsense."

"Really."

"I don't know what you mean."

"These old steps? Willa, if there's anything special about them . . ." Elsie pointed at the landing. "It has nothing to do with poetry."

"Elsie . . ."

"They're a product of human labor! Willa, someone had to mix this concrete! Then pour it! Someone has to maintain a clear path, sweep the leaves or shovel snow . . ."

"The *narrowest* possible way to think about it."

"Maybe," Elsie said. "Maybe not."

"No. I believe . . . I believe sacred spaces *do* exist in the world. With or without human intervention."

Charles Street had once been a self-contained block, like a well-made paragraph, a series of brick storefronts interspersed with well-kept residential facades. As Willa stood talking to Elsie near the stoop, she saw how out of balance the avenue had become. Several small, independent businesses had been demolished to make room for larger mercantile warehouses. The advent of the automobile had made widening the street necessary, squeezing pedestrians' desire lines. Now the nurses' dormitory attached to the Massachusetts Eye and Ear Infirmary threatened to pump dozens of new strollers into the crowds, like injecting a coagulant into a bloodstream, clotting it, causing, perhaps, an unintended infection, a dangerous swelling.

"So. Sacred spaces?" Elsie said to Willa, amused.

Willa smiled wistfully. "Coastal shorelines—anywhere. Preferably capped with lighthouses. The desert Southwest, first and foremost. New Mexico. When Edith and I went there, years ago, you should have seen it . . . oh, Elsie . . . the skies alive with lightning, rumbling like a drum, and the cliff dwellings, like little swallows' nests . . . they threw the thunder back at us, echoing up and down the canyons. I found so many shards of ancient pottery in the sand, instantly I felt connected to people of a bygone time. *That's* what I mean by 'sacred.'"

"Connected?"

"Yes . . . the sense that life is *big*, Elsie. Living's too damn much trouble unless you can get something big out of it." She looked away shyly, at the implacable black door. "I suppose that's laughable."

"I'm not laughing," Elsie said softly.

"You should go there. The desert. You'd see what I mean."

"Somehow, I don't think I'd react the way you did. *The Nation* just did a series of articles on Santa Fe—did you see them? Life is hard there. You know, for the Indians."

"Oh, the politics of the place don't interest me."

"But the people . . ."

"I'm talking about ancient spirits!"

"It seems so far away, the desert. Distant and grueling. I don't think I'd like it."

Now Elsie and Willa faced the door. Elsie: "No!"

"What's wrong?"

"*You* go in front of *me*! My god, I don't want to be *presented* to them like I'm an odd little gift to unwrap."

"Good heavens. So *sensitive*!" Willa laughed. But it was true: Willa thought of Elsie as her discovery, a bright young talent to set at the feet of her mentors.

And Elsie knew it.

This unspoken knowledge stood like a fence between them.

Willa primped her hair beneath her hat. "Do I look all right?"

"Splendid. Me?"

Willa frowned. "You'll do."

The women stood shoulder to shoulder now, still straightening themselves. Willa prepared to knock on the door. "When Dante passed through the gate—"

"Oh Willa, please!"

"It was his first step toward Paradise. He thought he heard singing . . . maybe it was just the gate clanging . . . or a chorus of angels . . ."

Elsie laughed. "Reels! Set!"

Willa blushed. It was so easy to tease her; she approached everything with the humorless bluntness of a prairie girl.

"So, when this door opens, we'll hear angels?" Elsie asked.

"I'm wondering if I should even take you in there with me."

"Willa." Elsie touched her friend's jacket. "Thank you for bringing me. Really. I'll behave."

"Honestly, Elsie, sometimes I can't tell if you're just being naughty or obtuse." Willa smoothed the girl's collar. "One of your rough charms, I suppose."

"Remember the day we met? I stood there in your office, thinking, 'This is a woman raised in the cornfields.' I could see it. Your ruddy color, perhaps. And I could tell you thought I was a foolish city girl who had stumbled toward your desk quite by accident. It wasn't until you introduced me to Mr. McClure and said to him, 'Miss Sergeant has brought in something on the sweated workers in the tenements. We must find her some more assignments' that I felt I might have a chance someday of winning your approval."

"Oh, Elsie, I've always known you were meant for something special." Willa flattened her palm against the door. "It's why I've wanted to bring you here. Once you step inside, I hope you'll feel, as I do, that nothing is, well . . . nothing is nobler than a life devoted to art. I know that sounds 'high-falutin,' as we used to say on the prairie . . . but it's what these fine ladies have taught me by their living example."

"I'm glad, Willa."

"In fact . . ."

"Yes?"

"When we return to New York, I plan to quit my editorial job."

"Willa!"

"I'll scale my life down, block off time . . ."

Elsie squeezed her friend's shoulder. "You'll write stories? Novels?"

"One's powers don't last forever."

Elsie hugged her.

"Soon these ladies' time will pass," Willa murmured. "Then it will be our turn, briefly. And after *that* . . ."

"Oh, Willa, we're going to change the world!" Elsie cried. For a long moment (though both women knew that, outside the boundaries of art, moments are never long), Willa and Elsie stood together in loving embrace, without the slightest understanding of each other.

Epilogue

In 1915, when Annie Fields passed away, 148 Charles Street was emptied, shuttered, and demolished—at her request. She could not bear the thought that, after her death, the house would be stripped of its signed first editions, its piano, its objets d'art, and redesigned for the more mundane purposes of child-rearing or feeding a contented stockbroker home from trading on the market. Conversely, she understood that no attempt to re-create the past would ever succeed. No ghost story competitions could match those of John Greenleaf Whitter and Harriet Beecher Stowe; no drawing room concertos could equal those of Ole Bull, whose name, unknown to modern audiences, would only elicit laughter now. As Willa wrote, "If we try to imagine [Mrs. Fields's] dinner parties . . . the scene is certainly not to us what it was to her: the lighting has changed, and the guests seem hundreds of years away from us. Their portraits no longer hang on the walls of our academies, nor are their 'works' much discussed." In fact, long before Mrs. Fields died, the second-floor library, which once provided a "seat for every visiting shade," in the words of Henry James, had become (James again) a "votive temple to memory"; in her late years, Mrs. Fields had taken to wearing widow's weeds of flowing purple and black, following, first, the death of her husband and then Miss Jewett's sorrowful passing.

The lot on which the house once stood was cleared to make way for an automobile garage.

By that time, Charles Street, widened on half a dozen occasions, had become a sooty thoroughfare. Developers had ploughed under riverside gardens to make room for large apartment squares featuring "splendid" views of the water. Individual medical clinics ("The smallest fevers gratefully received," said one quaint old sign) had given way to sterile complexes controlled by insurance outfits as far away as California. Luxury shops burgeoned where horses had once been stabled in structures older than the American Revolution. European immigrants displaced by war rushed to fill thin-walled rooms in the tenements that proliferated around the Back Bay. The great basin's cool and isolated sea presence, where quiet readers once took books on pleasant summer evenings, became a teeming, overheated ship-side bazaar, specializing in weaponry and contraband.

"Just how did this change come about, one wonders," Willa wrote. "When and where were the Arnolds overthrown and the Brownings devaluated? Was it at the Marne? At Versailles, when a new geography was being made on paper?"

No boundaries, insisted the Boston real estate firms, *No regulations! The dynamics of commerce must be free to spread as they will, enriching us all.* And yet nothing defined new development so much as fences and their legal equals, contracts and deeds.

One had to travel many thousands of miles, into the country's innermost regions, the snowy fields of Willa's childhood, the scorched deserts of Elsie's tests of self-reliance, to encounter open range. Something about these lands—Nebraska, the great Southwest—resisted enclosure, even when someone raised wires and posts to cordon off an acre. The vastness, perhaps, accounted for the negligible borders in these untamable plains, the puniness of attempts at possession.

It was only in a place like Charles Street, where the ratcheting of human activity had always been central, that the profundity of change could be appreciated or lamented. Only in a place where workers once worked, dancers once danced, readers once read—*and then they were no more*; only in a place where fences, legalities, and literary manifestos enforced the law—*and then they were no more*; only in such a place, like the lot on which a garage once stood, a garage that had, in its time, replaced a haven for artistic achievement, where two women once stood on a stoop together trying to fathom each other, and then, hand in hand, stepped across the threshold.

AUTHOR'S NOTE

To date six major biographies and two memoirs of Willa Cather have been published, though you would not necessarily know that the biographers were writing about the same woman.

148 Charles Street is a work of fiction. As such, it does not remain strictly faithful to known facts, chronologies, or biographies, all of which are tweaked and violated freely, within these pages, in service to the novel's narrative and themes. Nevertheless, the story tries to stay true to the spirits of the people on whom it is based, to the extent that I understand those spirits.

The text of this novel makes frequent reference—directly, indirectly, and obliquely—to the following works.

By Elizabeth Shepley Sergeant: *French Perspectives*; *Shadow-Shapes: The Journal of a Wounded Woman, October 1918–May 1919*; *Willa Cather: A Memoir*; "The Journal of a Mud House" in *Harper's*, 1922; "Dr. Jung: A Portrait" in *Harper's*, 1930.

By Willa Cather: *The Song of the Lark*; *My Ántonia*; *Death Comes for the Archbishop*; *A Lost Lady*; *The Professor's House*; *My Mortal Enemy*; *Shadows on the Rock*; *Not Under Forty*; "Behind the Singer Tower"; "Before Breakfast."

By Edith Lewis: *Willa Cather Living*.

By Andrew Jewell and Janis Stout, editors: *The Selected Letters of Willa Cather*.

By Carl Jung: "The Spiritual Problem of Modern Man."

By Paul Gauguin: *The Tahitian Journals*.

By Henry James: "Mr. and Mrs. James T. Fields" in the *Atlantic*, 1915.

The following scholarly/critical books and articles provided useful background information: Melissa J. Homestead, *The Only Wonderful Things: The Creative Partnership of Willa Cather and Edith Lewis*; Joseph Campbell, "Editor's Introduction" to *The Portable Jung*; Steven Trout, *Memorial Fictions: Willa Cather and the First World War*; Molly H. Mullin, *Culture in the Marketplace: Gender, Art, and Value in the American Southwest*; David Harrell, *From Mesa Verde to The Professor's House*; Margaret D. Jacobs, "Making Savages of Us All: White Women, Pueblo Indians, and the Controversy over Indian Dances in the 1920s"; Robin S. Walden, "The Pueblo Confederation's Political Wing: The All Indian Pueblo Council, 1920–1975"; Kenneth Dauber, "Pueblo Pottery and the Politics of Regional Identity"; Barbara Rotundo, "148 Charles Street"; Karen Cord Taylor, "Massachusetts Eye and Ear Selling Hotel/Garage" in the *Beacon Hill Times*; United States Department of the Interior, National Park Service, National Register of Historic Places, Registration Form, "Beacon Hill Historic District."

CPSIA information can be obtained
at www.ICGtesting.com
Printed in the USA
LVHW050707110222
710312LV00005B/9

9 781496 229748